**As soon as he'd laid eyes on Flora Gavia again, something had pulsed back to life inside him.**

A desire to engage again. Desire for a woman. Hunger.

The fact that it was *her* of all people was not entirely welcome, but Vittorio assured himself that even if she was up to something, he would be prepared.

A little voice reminded him that he'd felt something for her on the wedding day, when she'd appeared in that dress. He'd noticed her then. She'd made a mark, a mark that hadn't been made before. Because he hadn't noticed her previously. Or had deliberately chosen not to. Not wanting the distraction.

But now he was distracted. And he was going to do whatever it took to persuade her that he at least owed her sanctuary. As for anything more than that... He'd seen the way she blushed whenever he looked at her. They were both adults. If she was prepared to admit she felt the same chemistry as him, then perhaps this offer of sanctuary could become something much more mutually satisfying.

Irish author **Abby Green** ended a very glamorous career in film and TV—which really consisted of a lot of standing in the rain outside actors' trailers—to pursue her love of romance. After she'd bombarded Harlequin with manuscripts, they kindly accepted one, and an author was born. She lives in Dublin, Ireland, and loves any excuse for distraction. Visit abby-green.com or email abbygreenauthor@gmail.com.

**Books by Abby Green**

**Harlequin Presents**

*A Ring for the Spaniard's Revenge*
*His Housekeeper's Twin Baby Confession*
*Heir for His Empire*

***Jet-Set Billionaires***

*Their One-Night Rio Reunion*

***Passionately Ever After...***

*The Kiss She Claimed from the Greek*

***Princess Brides for Royal Brothers***

*Mistaken as His Royal Bride*

***Hot Winter Escapes***

*Claimed by the Crown Prince*

Visit the Author Profile page at Harlequin.com for more titles.

# "I DO" FOR REVENGE

ABBY GREEN

ISBN-13: 978-1-335-93917-3

"I Do" for Revenge

Harlequin Enterprises ULC
22 Adelaide St. West, 41st Floor
Toronto, Ontario M5H 4E3, Canada
www.Harlequin.com

Printed in Lithuania

# "I DO" FOR REVENGE

This is for Susan Drennan McGrath, aka Susie Q. She was right by my side during my quest for publication, encouraging and supporting me every step of the way, opening a bottle of bubbles to celebrate a rejection letter because it came with "notes"!

She never doubted I could succeed and 60+ books later, I still can't quite believe that I have. But she was right. Friends like this are rare and I'm incredibly lucky. Thank you, Susie Q. <3

# CHAPTER ONE

VITTORIO VITALE POURED himself a generous measure of whiskey. Irish. The best. He raised the glass to the view of Rome, bathed in early-afternoon golden sunlight. His domain. Finally. He took a sip of the golden drink and the liquid burnt a trail down his throat before settling in his belly, sending out a glow.

A glow of intense satisfaction. Today was the culmination of all of his—

He frowned when the buzzer on his desk sounded. He'd asked not to be disturbed under any circumstances.

Irritation needled over his skin. He pressed a button. 'Tommaso, I specifically requested—'

'Sorry, sir, I know. But…um…your— Wait a second! You can't just—'

The door to Vito's office swung open and a woman appeared on the threshold. His eyes widened. A woman in full wedding regalia. The white dress looked complicated and fussy, with a high neckline and long sleeves. Lace over lace. Stiff. Formal. The voluminous skirt filled the doorway.

Her face was bright pink. Hair sleek and pulled back. A veil was trailing from the top of her head. She clutched an extravagant bouquet in one hand; the flowers looked stiff. Even from here, Vito could see the whites of her knuckles.

His assistant appeared behind the woman. Vito sent him a look and said, 'It's fine, Tommaso.'

Vito put down his glass. He'd have to delay his celebration for a moment. He thought of the woman he'd arranged to meet later, one of Italy's most beautiful models. Tall, willowy, long dark hair like silk. Stunning body. He really didn't want this interruption to affect his plans.

But evidently he would have to deal with the woman he'd been due to marry, about two hours ago.

He flicked a glance at his watch and put out a hand. 'Miss Gavia. Please, come in.'

Flora Gavia was so angry she could barely see straight. Had Vittorio Vitale just looked at his watch? As if she was inconveniencing him? The man who she'd waited for in the vestibule of the church for an hour? Before realising with sickening inevitability that he wasn't coming?

The anger of her uncle was still palpable, his face mottled with rage—even more so after an aide had whispered something in his ear. He'd turned to Flora and screamed at her that it was all her fault, that everything was ruined. And just before he'd stormed off with his wife, her aunt, in tow, he'd said, 'What little use you were to me is now gone. You've been nothing but a burden and a drain for fourteen years. You're dead to me.'

In that moment, Flora had gone numb, putting her emotions on ice. It had been too huge to absorb that the people who had taken her in at just eight years old were effectively walking away from her, leaving her on her own.

But then something had broken through as the guests had filed out of the church whispering and staring at her—*anger*, at the man who'd done this to her. Vittorio Vitale.

And now she was here facing him and she was momentarily blinded by his sheer masculine beauty. Tall and broad. Powerfully muscular. He more resembled a prize athlete than a titan of industry. A billionaire.

Short, thick dark hair. Swept back from a high forehead. Bone structure that would make anyone weep with envy. Sharp blade of a nose. A hard jaw. And that mouth. When she'd first seen him she hadn't been able to take her eyes off his mouth. Lush and tauntingly sexual.

Much to her shock—because she was extremely sexually inexperienced—she'd imagined him doing things to her with that mouth. And that had been *so* unsettling because no other man had ever made her think of such things, and the marriage between them wasn't remotely based on romance. It was to be strictly business. Except there *was* no marriage. Because he'd stood her up.

Flora blinked. The anger surged back and it was disconcerting. She didn't get angry. She was generally well disposed to most people and situations, believing in good outcomes. And that people had good intentions. But in the case of Vittorio Vitale, it was blindingly obvious his intentions had been nefarious all along.

He didn't even look guilty or remotely contrite. He looked almost…bored. Dressed in plain dark trousers and a white shirt. Top button open, sleeves rolled up.

Flora shook her bouquet at him, scattering petals on the floor. 'You're not even dressed for a wedding. You never intended on marrying me, did you?’ That fact was becoming painfully obvious.

He came around his desk and perched on the edge, crossing his feet at the ankles and putting his hands in his pockets. He couldn’t have looked more louche.

He said, ‘Truthfully? No. It wasn’t cold feet.’

She looked around the office, taking it in for the first time. It was at the top of a sleek modern building right in the historical centre of Rome, which was saying something about the influence of the person who’d built something like this here.

Floor-to-ceiling windows on two sides framed amazing views of the ancient city. The iconic shape of the Colosseum was just visible in the distance.

Flora dragged in a ragged breath. Her head was spinning. She looked at him again and this time tried not to notice how gorgeous he was. Feeling bewildered now, more than anything, she asked, ‘Why?’

Vittorio’s jaw clenched. He looked as if he wasn’t going to say a word. She bit out, ‘I think I have a right to know.’

Vittorio took his hands out of his pockets and folded his arms. ‘That’s fair enough. What did your uncle tell you?’

Flora swallowed and remembered the tirade he’d subjected her to. ‘Not much.’ He’d never told her anything really.

Vittorio frowned. ‘Are you aware that your uncle’s business is disintegrating as we speak?’

Flora’s gut clenched. Her uncle *had* seemed more preoccupied than usual lately. Her aunt even less civil. They’d stop talking as soon as she walked into a room and rudely ask her if she wanted anything. The fact that she'd agreed to a marriage of convenience at her uncle's behest seemed to have been forgotten pretty quickly.

'No, I wasn't aware. I'm not privy to his business dealings.'

'You were privy to this marriage arrangement, weren't you? You were under no illusions. You knew you had a way out in six months if you wanted it. You had nothing to lose.'

She'd agreed to the marriage for lots of reason but also because there'd been the get-out clause after six months. She'd always felt indebted to her uncle for taking over her guardianship after her parents and younger brother had died, tragically. He'd put a roof over her head.

It hadn't been perfect by any means, but she'd been able to stay with family, and in one of the most beautiful cities in the world.

Her uncle could have left her to an institution, or boarding schools.

*But then he wouldn't have had access to your trust fund*, pointed out a little voice.

Flora reminded herself that he'd needed that money for her education and maintenance. To pay for the house staff to stay behind on holidays to watch her while they'd travelled around the world.

The fact that there was nothing left of her inheritance, according to her uncle, just showed how expensive it had been to take care of her. As he'd pointed out to her, this marriage was to be as much about protecting her future as for his benefit. He'd told her that he couldn't live with himself if anything happened and he couldn't provide for her or give her an inheritance. This marriage would protect them both.

She'd owed her uncle, for everything he'd done for her. But today that debt had ended in spectacular fashion.

'You asked for the six-month get-out clause,' Flora pointed out.

'My insurance in case things didn't go as planned, so I wouldn't be caught out. Your uncle didn't like it, but he didn't have much choice.'

*In case things didn't go as planned.*

Flora wasn't sure what that meant. The acute embarrassment hit her again. The anger resurfaced.

'How could you?' she demanded emotionally. 'How could you do something so heartless and cruel? Do you have any idea how it felt to stand there and wait? How humiliating?'

Vito looked at the woman before him. Something twisted a little in his gut. His conscience. So he did have one after all.

But then he felt something more disturbing. An awareness. Up to this point, because he'd known what he had planned, he hadn't engaged much with Flora Gavia, seeing no point in acting out a charade of courtship. And she'd seemed happy that he'd kept his distance. The engagement had been short in any case, only a month from announcement to today.

So, he hadn't really noticed her much, aided by the fact that she'd always seemed to hover on the edge of the room, or on the edge of a group, never planting herself in front of him, as most women did.

They'd had dinner together with her uncle and aunt,

but her uncle had dominated the conversation. All Vito had had was an impression of Flora that she was quiet and a little mousy. Brownish hair. Brownish eyes. Pretty… but unremarkable.

But suddenly, here in his office, she was transformed. Maybe it was the dress, fussy as it was. Maybe it was make-up. Her hair was pulled back and sleek, showing off her face. She had high cheekbones. And her eyes were much bigger than he remembered and not a dull brownish at all, but a startling shade of gold and brown. Long lashes.

Her mouth was far more lush than he recalled. Lush enough to make him stare. To wonder how on earth he'd missed this before. An electric charge sizzled in his blood.

His gaze drifted down over the dress, where her breasts moved up and down with her agitated breath. They were high and full. Small waist. Shapely hips. A classic feminine figure and one she'd kept hidden under shapeless clothes before now.

Basically she'd never made an impression. He'd never wanted to look twice. But now he was looking. Twice.

She shook the bouquet at him again. 'Well? Don't you have anything to say?'

Vito dragged his gaze back up. Petals were strewn all over his floor. Her veil was askew, and then, as if realising that, she made a face and pulled it from her head, throwing it down. Her sleek chignon was coming loose and Vito had the absurd urge to go over and loosen it completely so that her hair fell down over her shoulders.

He'd never seen it down and the fact that he noticed, and, worse, had a desire to see it down, was very irritating.

She said, 'Answer me. Please.'

Vito looked at her. There was a catch in her voice this time. His insides curdled. Was she going to cry? He went clammy at the thought, his head filled with unwelcome memories of his mother's grief-ravaged face. Unwelcome memories of not being able to fix her pain.

But Flora didn't look as if she was going to cry. She looked…confused.

Vito said, 'You really didn't know?' He didn't trust her as far as he could throw her. Clearly she was up to something, perhaps trying to salvage what she could out of the debacle unfolding for her uncle. He would play along for now.

She held up her hands, the bouquet beginning to look very frayed. 'Know what?'

The sense of triumph Vito had been feeling only a short time before was still palpable. 'As of today, coinciding with the wedding—'

'You mean *non*-wedding,' Flora pointed out.

Vito inclined his head. 'However you'd like to describe it. As of today, your uncle's business is in free fall and I now own most of his shares, enough to take control. He thought we were doing a deal. We weren't. I was. To crush him.'

Flora looked even more confused. She started to pace, trampling the veil under her feet, the bouquet an extension of one hand as she gesticulated. 'So what…? You're saying it was just a corporate takeover? Then why would you need a convenient marriage and why the theatrics?' She stopped and looked at him.

Years of anger and grief had calcified into a hard stone

in Vito's gut. 'Because this wasn't just about a corporate takeover, there was more to it. A lot more.'

Flora looked at him. She stabbed the air with the bouquet. 'Like what?'

Tension filled Vito. 'Like the fact that your uncle was responsible for ruining my father's business and ultimately for my father's suicide and my mother's subsequent death.'

Flora's hand with the bouquet dropped and the flowers slipped out of her hand to the floor, joining the veil. She swallowed visibly. 'I'm so sorry, that's awful. I had no idea.'

She looked stricken. Her acting ability irritated Vito. He straightened up and looked at her. Right now she embodied the Gavia family, and he despised them.

'Your uncle didn't even remember me when we met. My name didn't register. I was able to come in and decimate his business and social standing and not once did it occur to him that the name "Vitale" should mean something to him. That it should remind him of the man whose business he ruined from the inside out, causing my father to be accused of corruption, to lose his good name and standing. He almost went to jail, but at the last moment your uncle begged for mercy from the authorities, playing the saviour, when he'd been behind it all.'

He didn't mention the way he and his parents had been ostracised overnight, by friends and neighbours. How they'd lost their home. How his very first proper girlfriend had stopped taking his calls, and had soon reappeared hand in hand with one of Vito's best friends. The double betrayal had been immense. He'd learnt there and then that there was only one person you could rely on. Yourself.

Vito said grimly, 'Your family name and business go back generations, my father was the first in his family to make a real success of the business and your uncle saw him as a threat, which was ridiculous. Your uncle could have bought him off a hundred times over, but he went after him, for sport, and to let him know that his ambition was to be punished. My father died of shame, by his own hand.'

Flora's eyes were huge. 'And your mother...'

Vito was angry he'd exposed himself to this woman. That her eyes and the manufactured emotion were affecting him. He'd never sought sympathy in his life and certainly not now from a member of the family who had destroyed his.

He said in a clipped voice, 'She got sick and we didn't have the money to pay for private health care. She died while waiting for treatment. Treatment that could have saved her. That's all you need to know.'

Flora's anger drained away. She was shocked. And yet, at the same time, she wasn't shocked. Not any more. Not after her uncle had just cut her loose so brutally. Not after he'd so obviously used her in a business deal. 'I had no idea.'

Vittorio made a dismissive sound. 'Don't make a fool out of me. You might not have known my story, but you were as invested in this marriage as your uncle. That six-month get-out clause would have ensured your wealth for life. There was no downside for you.'

Flora looked at him. His beauty mocked her now, because it was cold and cynical.

Her uncle had already told her that if she exited at the six-months mark, that money would be his. She hadn't even cared. She'd seen it as a means to escape from a marriage in name only, if she'd needed it. The truth was that she'd agreed to the marriage primarily out of loyalty to her uncle but also for more complicated reasons. The fact that she'd found Vittorio Vitale totally fascinating. If unbelievably intimidating.

Somewhere, in a deep and shameful place, she'd known that a man like him would never choose a woman like her, and so she'd indulged in a little fantasy. Believing for a brief moment that when they married, perhaps a man who'd barely looked at her might look at her properly…see her as a woman.

The thought of anything more had felt far too audacious to even contemplate.

When he'd stood her up today, she'd been reminded in a very comprehensive and cruel way that nothing could incite a man like him to marry her. Not even a business deal. She'd even wondered if she'd been the one to ruin it all, just by not being alluring enough. Certainly her uncle had made her feel as though it had been her fault.

But it hadn't been because this man had never intended on following through with his part of the arrangement.

She said dully, 'I was just a pawn to try and maximise my uncle's downfall. The marriage plan was a particularly creative and cynical touch.'

It wasn't much comfort to know that she hadn't necessarily been instrumental in this process. It was almost more insulting. She really was that inconsequential.

Now Vittorio was sneering. 'Oh, please, spare me the self-pity. Your uncle was the one who suggested the marriage. He obviously saw an added bonus to going into business with me. Insurance for life. I won't deny I saw the benefits of embarrassing him socially when he handed me the opportunity. You were in it together, why on earth else would you have agreed to a marriage of convenience with a total stranger if it wasn't for your own benefit too?'

Flora clamped her mouth shut. She wasn't about to articulate to this cold, judgemental and vengeful man her complicated feelings of loyalty and gratitude to her uncle, a man who patently hadn't deserved any of it. If anyone was the fool here, it was her, the full extent of which was becoming horrifyingly clear.

No wonder her uncle had kept her inside like a hothouse flower for years, while all along planning on selling her off to the highest bidder. He'd been keeping her out of sight and away from any kind of influence. He'd even had her home-schooled!

She'd presumed he was just being overprotective and it had made her feel cared for. She felt nauseous now when everything began to make awful sense. Had she really been that starved for love and attention? Her twisting gut told her the answer. *Pathetic.*

Vittorio's excoriating look just flayed Flora further. She felt as if she'd lost three layers of skin. She muttered, 'I need to go.'

He put out a hand. 'By all means, you know where the door is.'

Flora turned and went towards the door, the dress moving stiffly around her. His cruel callousness stopped her though. She turned around again. 'I'm very sorry for what happened to you and I can understand your need to see justice done.'

She pointed to herself. 'This was not the way to do it though, far from it. What you did today reduced you to my uncle's level. You're just as mean and ruthless. You humiliated me for sport.'

For a moment he didn't react, then he said, 'Nothing happened to you today that you won't have forgotten about in a week. Believe me, I could have been far more ruthless with your uncle. He still has assets. He has a way back if he wants to work for it. And you have your own funds from your parents.'

Flora's mouth opened. 'How do you know about that?'

The fact that he obviously didn't know that her inheritance was already totally depleted was something she wasn't going to divulge. Sickeningly, a memory came back, of her uncle persuading her to sign a form allowing him access to her inheritance before she came of age—he'd told her it was for her benefit but after these revelations, she knew that that action had not been for her benefit. Her naivety made a hot flush of mortification rise up.

Vittorio shrugged. 'It came up when I was investigating your uncle. If anything you should be thanking me. You're free now to live your life, out from under your uncle's shadow. You're twenty-two, you have your inheritance. Today isn't the cash-in day you'd hoped for, but I've no doubt you can manufacture a strategic marriage all of your own, once everyone has moved on to the next salacious news story.'

Flora, somehow, found it within herself to push down the rising nausea and lift her chin. She said, 'You know what? I should have suspected something when you never pushed for us to meet alone or have a conversation. This is the most we've talked since we met. I thought you were just being a gentleman.'

Vittorio shook his head, eyes glittering like obsidian. Hard. Cold. 'I'm far from a gentleman.'

Flora hitched her chin higher. 'I know that now. And you're right about something else. I am free to live my life. I hope I never see you again.

'You—' she pointed at Vittorio with a trembling finger '—are not a nice person.'

Something caught her eye and impulsively she pulled the engagement ring he'd given her off her finger. It was a large, ostentatious diamond, in a gold setting with more diamonds either side. It weighed a ton. She resisted the urge to fling it at him, and put it down on a nearby table. 'You can have that knuckle-duster back. And by the way, I didn't mention it at the time because I didn't want you to feel bad, but you have no taste.'

It was probably the meanest thing Flora had ever said to anyone and she immediately felt awful, but before she could forget what this man—and her uncle—had put her through she turned and walked out.

Her dress took up most of the elevator as she descended and as she walked through the ground-floor lobby she willed the nausea to stay down and finally made it outside, sucking in lungfuls of air.

People stared as they walked past but she was oblivious. Panic now replaced the sense of nausea. She had nothing. No one. Nowhere to go. She was completely alone and she was only realising now that she'd been alone all along because her uncle and aunt had never really cared for her.

They'd taken her inheritance!

And that man back there? Flora couldn't imagine him caring for *anyone*. He was cruel, cold, heartless, ruthless, cynical, mean— She stopped. Took a breath. And realised that amidst the panic, there was also something far more fledgling rising up. A sense of…liberation.

Vittorio was right about one thing. She was free now. Totally free. Free of that sense of loyalty and obligation she'd had since her uncle had taken her in.

She looked around her as if seeing the world for the first time. She was on the precipice of something both terrifying and a little exhilarating. What would she do? Where did she go from here? The panic crept back, but she forced herself not to let it overwhelm her.

As she stood there on the pavement outside Vittorio's offices, in her wedding dress, with her hair coming loose, Flora said to herself, *Think. Think.* The first thing to do—find a bed for the night and get rid of this dress. And then…she would tackle tomorrow.

Flora turned left and set off, head held high, ignoring the looks and jeers from a group of young guys on mopeds. She would find a way. She would. She had to. She had no choice. There was no one she could ask for help. She was on her own now. And that was okay. She believed in the goodness of people—*most people*—and that good things would happen. With this blind faith guiding her, she disappeared into the streets of Rome, the train of her wedding dress trailing behind her.

Vito stood at his window for a long time, drink forgotten. He was unsettled by what had just happened.

*You think?* jeered a voice.

He ignored it. The truth was that his focus had been solely on Umberto Gavia for so long that when Gavia had proposed the marriage of convenience, Vito had gone along with it, seeing it purely as a bonus addition to his overall takedown of the man.

And, as Flora had never really made much of an impression, he'd found it easy not to think of her as a person, standing in a church waiting for him, because of course he'd always known he wouldn't be there.

But she hadn't known that. And he hadn't really thought of those consequences beyond the inevitable social embarrassment they'd cause Umberto Gavia. But now he did think of her. Because she'd stood right in front of him reminding him she was a consequence. A person who, if she was to be believed, hadn't had much of a clue as to what was going on.

And yet she'd agreed to the marriage. So he'd just assumed that she and her uncle were in cahoots. Therefore she'd deserved—

*What?* demanded a voice. *To be humiliated in front of Roman society? To be judged and punished like her uncle?*

*Yes.* A Gavia was a Gavia. It hadn't just been Vito's family that Umberto had decimated, it had been countless others. When Vito had looked into his practices to build his case against him, he'd found even more heinous acts committed against people.

But Flora hadn't just behaved like a cold-hearted Gavia. She hadn't come to him cajoling or begging or crying or looking for sympathy. She'd been angry. Confused. Bewildered. And she'd looked genuinely upset when he'd told her about his family.

Vito told himself he'd be an idiot not to suspect it had been an act. An attempt to salvage what she could for herself.

*You are not a nice person.*

Vito had never claimed to be *nice*. He'd stopped being nice right around the time when his mother had slipped away, her body ravaged by illness. That had been the moment when he'd set his sights on making sure that Umberto Gavia would one day pay for his actions.

And that day had come. He hardened his heart. Flora Gavia would be fine. She had a huge inheritance from her own parents—her father had been Umberto's brother.

*But he hadn't been involved in the family business, so why punish her?*

Vito pushed that aside. Her father might not have been directly involved, but she'd been brought up by Umberto since she was a child. She was practically his daughter.

No doubt he'd see her at a social function soon, looking for a replacement husband. Or, she'd have returned to join her uncle wherever he'd sloped off to.

*She would be fine.*

The Gavia family hadn't survived for generations without brass necks, and, as Vito had told Flora, he hadn't decimated Umberto Gavia as much as he could have. The man was badly wounded financially and socially, but he could return if he worked for it.

Vito knew that Umberto was essentially lazy though, so he didn't expect to see him around any time soon.

As for Flora… Vito had to admit reluctantly that he would be intrigued to see her again. The Flora who'd just accosted him here in his office had shown a far more intriguing side of herself. If Vito had met that woman before today…he might have felt very differently about leaving her standing at the altar.

But he had. And now it was done. He could move on. He picked up his drink and threw what remained of the whiskey down his throat. But somehow, this time, the glow of satisfaction felt a little dulled and a distinctly acidic aftertaste lingered in his mouth and stomach for a long time.

# CHAPTER TWO

*Six months later, Rome*

'VITALE! WHERE THE hell have you been?'

Vito forced a smile at the man who'd called at him. He made his way through the crowd of Rome's most monied and exclusive people in one of its oldest and most venerated hotels.

There had just been a charity auction at an annual fundraising event and people had paid eye-watering sums for things like yachts and Caribbean islands, all without batting an eyelid.

He used to take this scene for granted, but lately…he'd been finding such displays of wealth tedious.

A woman's hand landed on his arm. He looked down. Long perfect nails. Blood red. Perfectly tanned skin. The ubiquitous diamond bracelet. His nose wrinkled at the perfume. Too heavy. He looked up and registered a model whom he vaguely knew. Beautiful. Stunning. He waited for a beat.

*Nothing.*

He took her hand and lifted it from his arm. Her eyes widened. Immediately incensed. Vito moved on towards the man he knew. 'Roberto, *ciao*—'

At that moment, there was a loud crash, what sounded like a hundred glasses breaking and shattering. Vito looked around and saw the back of a waitress. She was bending down and trying to deal with the tray that had just fallen, spilling its contents of glasses.

He didn't take in much detail apart from her black skirt and white shirt. Brown/golden hair pulled up into a bun. A space had formed around her as if people were repelled by the scene. Something about that irritated Vito. He went over and bent down, picking up the larger pieces of glass.

She immediately said, 'Oh, please don't, I'll get into even more trouble.'

Something about her voice made him go still. He looked at her and even though her face was turned away, there was something about the curve of her cheek and jaw that made him stare.

As if aware of him staring, she looked at him. He saw her eyes widen and the colour leach from her face.

*Flora Gavia.*

Vito frowned, trying to take in what this was. Flora Gavia, an heiress, member of the hated family, dressed as a waitress at an event. *Not* dressed as a socialite.

'You…what…?'

Flora looked at something over his head and hissed, 'Please leave me alone.'

She muttered to herself as she continued picking up shattered glass. 'I'm in so much trouble. There's no way they'll take me on after this—'

Vito put his hand around her wrist. It felt unbelievably slender and delicate. Her scent hit him then too, floral with a hint of musk. Instantly pleasing.

She looked at him. 'What are you doing?'

He looked down. 'You're bleeding.'

She looked down to see blood seeping from a finger. She groaned. 'Now I'm really in for it. They *hate* blood.'

Before Vito could make sense of that, someone was arriving and apologising profusely. 'So sorry, sir, please, let us deal with this.'

Vito was all but pulled to standing by a veritable team of event staff who huddled around Flora and within seconds, like magic, she and the tray and all the broken glass were gone. The place was pristine again. For a second Vito wasn't even sure if he hadn't hallucinated it.

But then he noticed the slightly pink stain on the floor. Her blood. And that made him feel a surge of such a mix of emotions that he couldn't even name them. What he did feel was an urgency to go after her, to see if it really was her.

'Hey, Vitale, didn't that waitress look very like the Gavia woman you stood up at the altar?'

Vito looked at the man who'd come to stand beside him. He forced a smile again. 'I have to go, if you'll excuse me?'

Vito didn't wait for a response. He strode off the ballroom floor and out to the lobby. He stood there for a moment, not even sure where to start looking, but then he saw a figure with hair pulled up into a bun. Black skirt. A denim jacket over her shirt. A crossbody bag. Black sheer tights. Flat brogues.

She was walking quickly towards the entrance and Vito didn't think. He moved, and caught her just before she was about to disappear out of a side door. She looked up at him and went pale again. 'You.'

* * *

'Yes, me,' Vittorio Vitale said grimly, with his hand wrapped around her arm. Flora's finger was still throbbing under the makeshift tissue bandage but she was hardly aware. Of all the luck, and all the people she could have bumped into, it had to be him, in her moment of total and utter humiliation. She couldn't think of anyone who would get more out of this.

'Well?' she said pugnaciously. 'When you've stopped looking at me and getting pleasure out of seeing me scrabbling around the floor picking up broken glass in front of the most important people in Rome, I'd like to get on.'

If anything, the man looked even more gorgeous than Flora remembered. He was dressed in a classic black tuxedo and the material did little to disguise his powerful body. She could see the bunched muscle of his biceps and felt a little woozy.

*Lack of blood.*

That was it.

He was shaking his head. 'What are you doing here?'

She looked at him and then gestured at herself with her free hand. 'Do I really need to spell it out?'

He didn't answer, he just looked over her head and then tugged her with him, across the lobby to the reception desk, where a manager jumped to attention, barely glancing at her. 'Signore Vitale, how can I help you?'

'I'd like a room, please.'

Flora's mouth dropped open as she watched the manager issue Vittorio with a room key without so much as an eye-flicker. Now he was leading her across the lobby to the elevator. They were inside the small but luxurious space before Flora pulled her arm free and found her voice. 'What on earth do you think you're doing?'

Vittorio stabbed at a button. He said, 'That's what I'd like to ask you.'

Flora said, 'As it happens, before you accosted me I was going home because I've just lost my job. Tonight was part of a month's trial, and I failed.'

Vittorio looked at her as the elevator ascended. 'Since when are you working as a waitress?'

Flora pretended to look at her watch and said tartly, 'As of about ten minutes ago I'm no longer a waitress. It was a short-lived career.'

The elevator doors opened onto a quiet corridor with plush cream carpets, soft lighting and walls painted in hues of cream and gold.

Vittorio stepped out but kept a hand on the door, stopping it from closing again. He sounded impatient. 'Please, Flora, I think we need to talk.'

'About what? I think we said all that needed to be said on the day you stood me up at our wedding.'

A muscle in his jaw pulsed. The muted sound of voices came from nearby. He glanced away and Flora had an urge to smack his hand aside and quickly press the button to escape but at that moment an elegant older couple appeared.

The woman smiled at Flora and even though Flora was being offered an opportunity to use this couple as an excuse to stay in the elevator and travel back down, something else inside her compelled her to step into the corridor, out of their way, signalling that she was with Vittorio, even though she couldn't have looked more mismatched with her white shirt, black skirt and serviceable shoes.

The doors closed again and Vittorio was heading for a doorway at the end of the corridor. Flora followed him, her feet sinking into the carpet. It had been months since she'd inhabited surroundings as salubrious—not that her uncle's palazzo had even been that luxurious. It hadn't been comfortable. It had been more like a museum, stuffed with antiques and forbidding portraits of ancestors who looked nothing like her.

Flora had taken after her English mother's side of the family, perhaps something else that had never endeared her to her uncle.

Vittorio was standing in the open doorway now and looking at her as he undid his bow tie with his other hand. He cut a rakish figure with stubble lining his jaw.

Before taking a step over the threshold Flora commented, 'You obviously do this a lot.'

'What?'

'That manager didn't even blink when you asked for a room.'

Vittorio's mouth quirked ever so slightly on one side. 'That's probably because, as of about a month ago, I own this hotel.'

'Oh.' Flora felt exposed. She'd been imagining that it was a regular occurrence for Vittorio Vitale to appear with a woman demanding a room at short notice. As if he would do that with a woman like her!

He stood back. 'Please, come in.'

Flora took a breath and walked past him. His scent tickled her nostrils, sharp and musky with woodier undertones. All at once sophisticated but also with an edge of something indefinable. Very masculine.

She was very conscious of her own scent—eau-de-kitchen.

The room was palatial. Then she saw more rooms leading off this main one. It was a suite. With windows looking out over Rome. Flora could see a terrace outside.

She saw Vittorio reflected in the window, behind her. Tall and indistinct. She forced herself to turn around. 'Why do you want to talk to me?'

His bow tie was undone now. Top button open. He spread his hands out. 'What are you doing here like this? Why aren't you with your uncle? I heard he was last seen in South America trying to make a name for himself where he's less known.'

That stung. Vittorio knew more than she did. Her uncle hadn't been in touch since that morning at the church.

Feeling hurt and hating that weakness, she said, 'What my uncle does now, or where he is, is none of my concern. I haven't seen him since that morning six months ago.'

Vittorio's brows snapped together. 'What?'

Flora shrugged. 'It's like you said, I was free. I did my own thing.'

'What was that exactly…that has led you to this?'

The humiliation of his very public abandonment and the way he'd cast her out of his office as if she was nothing but an irritation made her say, 'You know what? I don't owe you any explanations. If you don't mind, I have somewhere to be and I need to go.' Because it was going to take her at least an hour to get back to where she lived on the outskirts of the city.

She moved back towards the door and Vittorio asked

incredulously, 'You really burnt through your inheritance that quickly?'

Flora stopped. Didn't turn around. She felt like laughing and crying all at once. The inheritance she'd never seen! Because her uncle had taken it. The truly pathetic part was that she'd never really known how much was there. She'd been too young to know at first and whenever she'd brought it up, her uncle had been vague and assured her he was taking care of it for her. No doubt this man, Vittorio Vitale, who had rebuilt his family's name and fortune, would laugh himself silly if he knew the full extent of her sad story.

As frigidly as she could, she said, 'Yes, that's exactly it. I squandered it and now I'm working in menial jobs. Goodbye, Vittorio, have a nice life.'

She was almost at the door when Vito broke out of his trance and said, 'Wait.' He was reeling. Nothing made sense. He knew something was very off but he wasn't sure what it was.

Flora stopped. There was something fragile about her from the back. Her hair pulled up into a high bun. He realised that she'd lost weight. He had a strong aversion to letting her out of his sight. He put it down to needing to know what she was up to, because it was something. Even if it didn't involve her uncle.

'Look, can I offer you something to eat? Drink?'

For a long moment she didn't move and then she turned around. She'd definitely lost weight. He could see it now. Even as he also noticed the same curves he'd noticed before, when she'd been in that wedding dress. Breasts high and full.

His body tightened in response.

*Not appropriate.*

It hadn't been then, and it wasn't now.

She said, 'Actually, maybe a sandwich, please.' Then almost as an afterthought, she said, 'And some sausages, if that's okay.'

Vito picked up the phone and made a call, then put it down again. She was hovering by the door, still in her jacket. 'Sit down, Flora. Make yourself comfortable. Can I get you something to drink?'

With almost palpable reluctance she came back in and perched on the edge of one of the sofas. *Not* the reaction Vito was used to from women.

'A glass of water, thank you.'

Vito went to the lavishly stocked mini-bar and took out some water for her and a small bottle of whiskey for himself. He put the drinks in glasses and came back over, handing her the water. He said, 'If you want something stronger, let me know.'

She shook her head. 'No, this is fine, thank you.' She took a gulp of water.

Vito noticed something and cursed softly. 'You're still bleeding.'

She lifted her hand and blood was trickling down her finger. 'I'm sorry, I didn't realise—'

Vito was already on the phone issuing an order. He put the phone back down and said, 'Come into the bathroom, let me see it.'

Flora was rummaging through her bag clearly looking for something. 'It's fine, I have another tissue here somewhere—'

'Flora—'

Her head came up and she looked at him.

He said, 'Let me see it, please.'

Flora lifted off her bag and stood up. Vito went into the bathroom and turned on the light. She followed him in.

He said, 'Give me your jacket.'

She slipped it off and he draped it over the back of the door. Then he took her hand in his and peeled off the makeshift tissue bandage. He muttered, 'Didn't they have any plasters?'

'I didn't hang around to find out. The boss was *so* angry.'

Vito looked at Flora. This close, he could see freckles across her nose. It felt curiously intimate. Her cheeks went a little pink. *She wanted him.* Vito was used to women wanting him but this was different. He sensed she'd never admit it, never mind use it.

She said, 'What is it? Have I got something on my face?'

Once again he was struck by how…pretty she was. With no make-up or adornment. Huge eyes. Long lashes. Those cheekbones. A mouth that was pure provocation, lips full and soft.

*How had he not noticed before?*

He knew how—because he'd been so fixated on her uncle.

He shook his head. 'No, there's just something…different about you.'

With visible self-consciousness, she touched her head with her free hand. 'It's probably my hair. I don't straighten it any more. Can't afford to. And I never could do it myself.'

Vito could see that it looked a little wild, with curly tendrils close to her hairline. He curbed the urge to free it and see it spill over her shoulders. He turned on the cold tap and put her finger under the water, hearing her intake of breath.

There was a knock on the door outside. Vito said, 'Hold it there until I get back.'

He could have sworn he heard a muttered *'yes, sir'*, but he went out and opened the door and admitted the room-service attendant who had arrived with a trolley containing the food and a first-aid kit.

Vito thanked him and tipped him and brought the first-aid kit into the bathroom, where Flora was still dutifully holding her injured finger under the water. He turned off the tap and dried her hand with a small towel, careful to be gentle.

He noticed her nails were short. Unvarnished. He took a plaster from the kit and placed it over the cut, saying, 'It was deep.'

Flora said, 'Thank you. You didn't have to do that.'

Vittorio threw away the wrapping and closed up the box. 'It was nothing.'

Impressed by his practicality, she asked, 'Where did you learn to do that?'

He looked at her, amused. 'Put on a plaster?'

She flushed. 'Some people are squeamish.' She remembered cutting her leg badly on barbed wire when she'd been smaller and going to her aunt. Her aunt had almost fainted on the spot, causing such a commotion that her uncle had had the house staff attend to her aunt before they'd even noticed that Flora was the one who required urgent attention. She'd ended up in hospital needing stitches.

She took her hand back, cradling it to her chest. It suddenly felt as if there were no air in the room. But before Flora could move or say something, Vittorio said, 'My mother was ill, as I mentioned before. I nursed her for a time. Medical stuff doesn't make me squeamish.'

Flora recalled what he'd told her about his parents. The reason for his revenge mission on her uncle. She could empathise.

Vittorio said, 'The food is here. You should eat.'

*Food.*

Flora's stomach rumbled faintly. It was the reason she'd stayed. Because she'd learned in the last few months not to look a gift horse in the mouth. She wasn't too proud to accept food, especially when it wasn't just her she had to think about.

She followed Vittorio back out to the suite. He'd taken off his jacket and his back was broad under the shirt, tapering down to slim hips. The trousers did little to hide the definition of his muscular buttocks.

He was standing at a trolley and lifting a silver domed lid from a plate. Flora's eyes went wide. A toasted sandwich with fries. Sausages on the side. She'd never seen anything that looked so delicious.

Vittorio put the plate of food on the table and pulled out a chair. 'Please, sit.'

Flora did. She picked up a chip and popped it into her mouth, almost closing her eyes at the salty tastiness. She noticed that there was no other food. 'Aren't you hungry too?'

Vittorio shook his head. 'I'm fine.'

Flora picked up the sandwich and was about to take a big bite out of it when she stopped. 'Can you not look at me? You're making me feel like an animal in the zoo.' In fairness, she conceded, he probably wasn't used to the spectacle of women actually eating in front of him. Her aunt had eaten like a bird and only Flora and the staff had known of the midnight trips to the palazzo kitchen where she would binge periodically, out of sight.

Vittorio looked at his watch. 'Actually, I need to speak to someone downstairs. I'll let you eat in peace.'

Flora felt a surge of relief not to be pinned under that obsidian gaze for a minute. He started walking to the door and then stopped and turned back. 'You'll be here when I get back.' It wasn't really a question.

She said, 'I do have to leave soon.'

'I won't be long, a few minutes. And then I can take you wherever you need to go.'

Flora immediately balked at the thought of him seeing where she was staying. 'Oh, no, that's fine, but I'll wait until you come back.'

He left and Flora took advantage of the privacy to polish off the sandwich and fries. She drank the water. And carefully wrapped up the sausages in a napkin.

When she was finished she put her jacket back on so she'd be ready to go when Vittorio got back. She would thank him for his hospitality and leave and go back to a world where he didn't exist. And hopefully she wouldn't have any more unnerving encounters with him. He stirred up way too much inside her.

* * *

When Vito returned to the suite it was empty. He felt an instant sense of panic mixed with regret mixed with irritation.

*Disappointment.*

He hadn't met many people he could trust and there was no reason why Flora Gavia would be any different.

But then he noticed that the French doors were open, leading out onto the balcony where a figure stood at the wall, and he felt exposed for his initial reaction. Why should he even care if Flora Gavia disappeared into the ether again?

*Because he wanted to know what was going on.*

He had the same slightly unsettling sense that he'd had the day she'd walked out of his office in the wedding dress—that he'd missed something huge and vital. Then, he'd reassured himself that it was nothing. He was just used to having all the information and leaving nothing to chance. He hadn't expected her to confront him on the day of the wedding.

She'd walked out of his office leaving more questions than answers. And now there were even more questions. Vito didn't like loose ends or things that didn't make sense. That was how you got caught out.

The fact that Flora Gavia was working as a waitress for an event company and that at least one person had recognised her was a potential problem. Perhaps it was part of a plan with her uncle. Perhaps she *was* now working solo, but until Vito knew for sure he'd have to keep her close.

# CHAPTER THREE

FLORA WAS MESMERISED by the view of Rome from this vantage point. She was so engrossed she didn't hear Vittorio return and nearly jumped out of her skin when he said from behind her, 'Your hair is down.'

She whirled around to see a look of shock on his face. She put her hands to her head. *This* was why her aunt had insisted on her keeping it straight when out in public. Its natural state was curly and wayward and untameable. Untidy.

'I took it down because my head was sore.' She started bundling it up again but Vittorio put out a hand.

'No, stop.'

She did. Dropped her hands. She realised now that he didn't look shocked, disgusted. He looked shocked, transfixed. She felt a swooping sensation in her belly.

He said, 'It's...beautiful.'

Flora felt heat come into her face. She was glad of the darkness. 'Thank you. It was my mother's... I mean, I inherited it from her.'

'Your mother was English.'

'Yes. My father was...Italian.' Obviously. Her father had been her uncle's brother. She felt seriously woolly-headed around this man.

She said, 'I should go. I really need to get back.'

'You have a boyfriend?'

Flora's eyes nearly bugged out of her head. The thought of having had the luxury of time to have a boyfriend was almost comical. She shook her head. 'No, no boyfriend but I do have responsibilities and where I live…it's a little bit different. I have to be back—' She stopped. Vittorio Vitale didn't need to know the minutiae of her living arrangements.

She said, 'Look, I just need to go now, okay? Thanks for the food…and for—'

'Losing you your job?'

She looked at him, surprised. 'It wasn't your fault. I dropped the tray.' Well, it had been a little his fault, she'd heard someone call his name and had seen him and she'd been in such shock that she hadn't looked where she was going and had bumped into something. But she wasn't about to reveal that.

'If I hadn't tried to help you it might not have been so bad.'

Flora made a face. 'Perhaps. Although, my track record for holding trays wasn't great to begin with. That was the third one I've dropped.'

'Ah,' Vittorio said.

'Funnily enough my uncle didn't consider learning how to hold trays full of glasses to be of importance in my schooling.'

'And yet that's what you're doing.'

Vittorio sounded curious. Flora went back into the suite. 'I just need to get my bag and then I'll be gone.'

'I'll give you a lift.'

Flora was putting her cross-body bag over her head

of unruly hair. She tensed. 'That's really not necessary, I'm out on the edges of the city.'

'I insist. I want to make sure you get home safely.'

Flora thought quickly. Maybe she could get him to drop her off somewhere nearby so he wouldn't see where she actually lived.

'Okay, then, if you insist.'

'My car is downstairs, let's go.' He picked up his jacket on the way and led her back out of the suite, to the elevator and down to the lobby. In the lobby though, Flora froze. Her event manager boss was also in the lobby and had seen her.

Vittorio saw her reaction and said sharply, 'Who is that?'

Flora said miserably, 'My now ex-boss.'

Vittorio said, 'Wait here.' And he walked over to the man, who Flora could see was going pale in the face. There were a few words exchanged, mostly on Vittorio's side, and the man was now going red and nodding frantically.

Vittorio came back and took her arm in his hand, guiding her out of the hotel through the main entrance. She looked back at her ex-boss, who appeared to be in some kind of shock.

They were outside the hotel now, going down steps to where a low-slung silver bullet of a car was waiting. A young valet was holding open the passenger door and Flora got in gingerly, feeling awkward, having to contort herself a little. The door closed.

Vittorio got in on the other side, deftly starting the car and manoeuvring them out into the Rome traffic. Flora gave him a general address of where she was staying.

She didn't want to distract him further but curiosity overcame her and when there was a lull in traffic she asked, 'What did you say to him?'

Vittorio was looking ahead, and Flora took in his strong profile. The man didn't have a bad angle.

He said, 'I told him that I didn't appreciate the way he treated his staff and unless he demonstrated a less punitive work environment in future, I wouldn't have him manage an event at my hotel again.'

'Oh.' Flora absorbed this. Not what she might have expected of the man who had been ruthless enough to ruin her uncle and stand her up on their wedding day. She also hadn't expected his hospitality. Or how gentle he'd been tending to her finger. The plaster was wrapped around it snugly. It was no longer throbbing, or bleeding.

He drove with easy confidence. Fast, but not too fast. He didn't need to show off. Her uncle had always terrified Flora with the way he drove.

Before she realised it they were in the quieter residential areas of Rome. Exactly where Flora had directed Vittorio. He said, 'Where now?'

'You can just let me out anywhere here.'

Vittorio was driving slowly and looking at the very sleepy/closed apartment blocks. 'Tell me which one. I'm dropping you to the door, Flora.'

*Flora.*

The way he said her name gave her flutters. She could sense he wasn't going to take no for an answer. She sighed and gave him the address. It was around the corner.

He pulled up outside and got out before she could move, opening her door. The entrance to where she stayed was a nondescript gate. Flora stood in front of it, feeling awkward. Vittorio loomed large under the street lights. It made her even more conscious of what was behind her.

She said, 'Okay, look, thank you for the lift. I can take it from here.'

He was frowning though and looking over her shoulder. 'What is this place? Some sort of…hostel?'

She seized on that. 'Yes, it's a hostel and guests aren't welcome inside.'

At that moment the gate opened behind Flora. An older woman stepped out. 'Flora? Are you okay?'

Flora nodded. 'Fine, Maria, this…er…gentleman was just dropping me home.'

'Okay. Because we need to talk, Flora. I'm afraid that it's not going to be possible for you to stay if you want to keep Benji here too.'

'Who's Benji?'

Vittorio's question couldn't distract Flora from the stomach-dropping panic she felt. She'd known this was coming but still…

Maria's voice was dry. 'Benji is Flora's baby.'

Vittorio stared at her. 'You have a baby? How on earth…? You were pregnant when we were due to get married?'

Maria barked out a laugh. 'Not a real baby.'

Flora put up her hands. 'Stop. Both of you.' She looked at Maria and turned her back on Vittorio. 'When do I need to move out?'

Maria's expression was soft, kind, but regretful. 'Probably as soon as you can. The inspectors could turn up any day now and if they find Benji…'

‘I know. And the last thing I want to do is get any of you into trouble, when you’re doing such amazing work.’

‘Work…what work?’ Vittorio asked.

Before Flora could answer, Maria said, ‘Who is this man? Can you trust him?’

‘With this information? Yes, I believe so…’

‘Okay, well, I’ll leave you to talk and then we can figure out where you’re going to go.’

Flora felt weary. ‘Okay, thanks, Maria.’

The other woman went back inside, shutting the gate securely again. Flora looked at Vittorio. His arms were folded. He wasn’t moving until he got answers.

First question. ‘What is this place? It’s not just a hostel, is it?’

Flora shook her head. ‘It’s a women’s aid centre, so I’m sure you can appreciate the need for sensitivity and discretion.’

‘What on earth are you doing in a women’s aid centre…?’ His brows snapped together. ‘Did someone do something? Did something happen?’

‘No, nothing like that. I ended up here…through somewhere else and they let me stay for a miminal fee. I worked for them to help out.’

‘You ended up here…?’

Flora swallowed. ‘Look, it’s really none of your concern. You should go.’

One thing Vito was very sure of was that he was going nowhere until he’d got to the bottom of why Flora was living in a women’s aid centre.

He said, ‘Who, or what, is Benji?’

Flora looked as if she was going to argue but then she said, 'Okay, fine, wait here. I'll be back.'

Vittorio leaned back against his car. It was quiet here. Residential. Nondescript. The perfect place for a women's aid centre. He could appreciate that. Flora was gone for about ten minutes and Vito was just appreciating the fact that no one ever kept him waiting when she reappeared with a bundle of what looked like scraggy fur in her arms.

'This is Benji. I found him in a skip a few weeks ago. He's blind in one eye.'

It was a dog. A puppy. Of indeterminate breed. Beagle-ish. With white and grey and a bit of brown. One brown eye and the other one was cloudy. The dog was curled trustingly against Flora's chest. Vittorio put out a hand to stroke him and the dog's hair went up and he growled, which sounded a little comical coming from something so small.

Flora said unapologetically, 'Sorry, he doesn't like men much.'

Vito pulled back his hand. 'Fair enough.'

He thought of what the woman had said. 'You have to move out because of the dog?'

Flora nodded. 'No animals allowed. They just don't have the facilities but it's heartbreaking because a lot of the kids who come here have had to leave pets at home. There isn't space for a garden. They really need to move to a better facility but they can't afford it.'

'What are you going to do?' Even as he asked the question, a plan started to formulate in Vito's head.

Flora bit her lip and Vito wanted to go over and tug it loose, press his own mouth against hers. Slip his hand under all that hair and tug it so that her head fell back, giving him deeper access to her—

'I'm not sure. Maybe Maria will know someone.'

'You're coming home with me.'

Flora looked at him. The colour drained from her face. 'That's preposterous.'

'If we'd got married, you'd be living with me now.'

'Well, that never happened because you stood me up, remember? And even if we had married, we'd be getting divorced now. Six months have passed.'

'You never know, you might have found me easy to live with and decided not to get divorced.'

Flora smiled sweetly. 'The same goes for you—you might have found me too irresistible to let go.'

Neither said anything for a moment and then Vito saw some colour come back into Flora's cheeks. He took advantage of what he knew. 'What if the inspectors turn up tomorrow? You don't want to be the cause of getting the centre shut down.'

Now she looked stricken. 'Of course not.'

'Then if you leave with me tonight, you'll be ensuring their safety.'

She looked tortured. It was almost insulting. But then from the moment she'd stormed into his office in the wedding dress, *no*, from the moment they'd met, she'd never shown much of an inclination to spend time with him. He couldn't remember a time when a woman had been so uninterested. From the age of puberty, Vito had known that he possessed a rare power. He'd never taken it for granted but he'd used it to his advantage when he'd had to.

She looked at him and Vito was struck again by her huge eyes. Her hair curled wildly, falling over her shoulders.

'Okay, but just for one night, and then I'll sort something out. Okay?'

Vito shrugged. 'Sure.'

'I'll go in and get my things. I won't be long. I have a carrier for Benji.'

'Do you need help?' Vito stood up straight.

She shook her head. 'No, it's better if you don't come in. Strangers, especially male strangers, aren't exactly… welcome.'

Vito put his hands in his pockets. He was rarely in a situation where he was ineffectual. It was eye-opening.

Approximately ten minutes later, Flora reappeared with a wheelie case in one hand and a pet carrier in the other. She handed Vito the wheelie case and said, 'I'll sit in the back with Benji so he doesn't get scared.'

Vito stowed the case. 'I've put in a call to my housekeeper to ensure there are provisions for a dog, and some food.'

'Thank you.'

Driving back into the city, Vito glanced in the rearview mirror and caught Flora's eye. For the first time since seeing her again he noticed shadows under her eyes like delicate bruises. He felt a clutch of something unfamiliar in his gut. Unfamiliar but not unknown.

*Concern.*

For a Gavia of all people.

Conflicting emotions tangled together, and the suspicion that he was being monumentally naive not to suspect that this woman was up to something. He needed to find out what was going on. 'So how did you end up in the women's aid centre?'

He glanced at her in the rear-view mirror again and she was avoiding his eye, biting her lip. Then their eyes met again and he felt it like an electric shock. His hands gripped the wheel tighter.

With almost palpable reluctance she said, 'I, er…was in a hostel in the city and someone mentioned the aid centre, that they were looking for a volunteer to help out and that there was a place to stay, if you did.'

Vito frowned. 'Hostel…what kind of hostel?'

'A homeless hostel.'

It took a second for that to sink in and when it did, Vito almost crashed the car. He swerved and a driver shouted expletives at him. He pulled into a layby and turned to face Flora.

He said one word. 'Explain.'

'Do we have to do this here? It might be better when you're not driving.'

'I'm not driving,' he pointed out. And then, 'Are you saying you were homeless?'

'Only for a couple of days.'

Vito couldn't sit there. He got out of the car, pulling his jacket off and throwing it aside. He felt constricted. He opened the passenger door and pulled the seat forward and said, 'We need to talk.'

They were on a quiet leafy street on the way back into the city, the moon shining bright. She got out. The dog made a little pitiful sound and she said something reassuring. For a bizarre moment Vito almost…envied the dog. Ridiculous.

Flora stood and faced him.

Vito folded his arms. 'Tell me everything that happened after you walked out of my office.'

Flora gulped. She might have imagined this scene in her weaker moments when she would have enjoyed seeing Vittorio Vitale grovelling a little, but now that he was in front of her looking positively…nuclear, it didn't feel as good as she might have imagined. She almost felt as though she should be apologising.

'When I left your office I had nothing. Nowhere to go. Not a cent of money.'

Vittorio shook his head. 'How?'

'I told you I hadn't seen my uncle since that day. He told me in no uncertain terms that any use I'd had was no longer valid. I did try to go to the palazzo but it was already closed up.'

'But what about your inheritance?'

Flora shook her head. 'My uncle plundered it over the years. I stupidly signed a form granting him access until I was of age.'

'In all the investigations we did, no one noticed that it was gone.'

'Well, it was.'

Vittorio sounded grim. 'He must have doctored the accounts. I had no idea you were destitute. I assumed you had that money, or that you'd just leave with your uncle.'

Flora repressed a shiver. 'No way.'

Vittorio cursed softly. 'You're cold. Let's go.'

She wasn't cold but he was already ushering her back into the car and closing the door and within seconds they were driving again, until they entered the historic centre of Rome. Not far from Vittorio's offices and where her uncle's palazzo had been.

Vittorio came to a stop outside a discreet building. A doorman jumped out and took Vittorio's keys. Another attendant took Flora's battered case and Vittorio said, 'Does the dog need to be taken around the block? Damiano can do it.'

Flora took Benji out of the carrier and attached his lead, handing it to the young man. She said, 'Thank you.'

The little dog trotted off happily. Vittorio said, 'He obviously doesn't dislike all men.'

Now Flora felt irrationally guilty. 'Um…no…mainly just the tall ones.' Who looked intimidating. She kept that to herself.

Inside, the apartment building was sleek and modern, belying the older exterior, which she figured must be protected as a lot of structures were in Rome. Vittorio obviously favoured a less traditional aesthetic, and, having grown up in the stuffy Gavia palazzo, Flora found she appreciated the clean lines.

They ascended in the elevator, Flora very conscious of still being in her waitress uniform. The doors opened directly into the apartment, a reception hall with marbled floors and a massive round table upon which sat a vase full of colourful blooms.

The apartment seemed to take up the entire top floor with massive rooms, tall ceilings and an outdoor terrace. A housekeeper met them, an older woman, Sofia. She showed Flora a dog bed and bowls for food and water and assured her they'd have more things tomorrow.

Flora was about to protest that they probably wouldn't

still be here but Vittorio was saying, 'Come into the living room. It's more comfortable.'

The room was filled with couches and chairs. Coffee tables stacked with books. Modern art on the walls. Muted colours. It was soothing. Flora had an urge to curl up on a couch and sleep for a week. She tried to hold back a yawn.

Vittorio was looking at her. He said, 'You should go to bed. You're exhausted.'

She didn't protest. As much because she *was* exhausted but also because she needed to try and absorb everything that had happened this evening since she'd heard someone say his name at that function, causing a chain of events leading to here.

Vittorio instructed Sofia to show Flora to her room and she dutifully followed the older woman down a series of corridors, to a door. Inside was a massive bedroom suite with dressing room and en suite. Even a living room with TV.

Sofia showed her where her case had been stowed and where there was a robe and toiletries. The woman's kindness made Flora feel emotional. After growing up in the sterile environment of her uncle and aunt's guardianship, she'd experienced more compassion and kindness in the last six months than ever before in her life. And from people who had the least amount of resources.

And yet… Vittorio had shown her kindness this evening. Disconcerting. The last person she would have expected to help her. She would have assumed if he'd seen her waitressing like that he'd either laugh or completely ignore her. Step over her as she'd picked up the broken glass. But he hadn't done anything of the sort. He'd stood up for her.

And now he was taking her in.

Flora's head was starting to throb. When Sofia had left, she explored the suite, and the lure of the luxurious marble bathroom was too much. She stripped off and stepped into a shower the size of a room and almost groaned with pleasure as steaming hot water sluiced down over her body.

She hadn't experienced this level of a shower in months, or actually ever, because the plumbing in the Gavia palazzo had been about the same age as the palazzo. So this was…heaven. She even succumbed to the lure to wash her hair, an epic feat at the best of times.

When her aunt had first seen her hair in all its natural glory when she'd been a child, she'd been so horrified that she'd made sure that it was always straight, ensuring Flora was subjected to rigorous hair-drying and straightening by a member of staff at least once a week.

When Flora emerged from the bathroom, swathed in a robe and with a towel wrapped around her head, she lay on the bed, promising herself she'd just have a quick rest before she finished drying off. But then her eyes closed and the throbbing in her head finally stopped and everything went blissfully dark and quiet.

Vito was pacing back and forth on his terrace. The dog had been returned to the apartment and was now sniffing on the terrace, stopping to wee on a plant every now and then. It had started howling when it had realised Flora was nowhere to be seen and so Vito had risked a bite, scooping the animal up into his arms, to try and keep him quiet. The dog had looked at him suspiciously for a long moment, nose twitching, and had then promptly curled into a ball in his arms. Until he'd squirmed to be put down again.

Vito's head was reeling.

*Was Flora telling the truth?*

His gut told him the answer. Why on earth would she have gone to such elaborate lengths on the off chance she'd run into him again to play on his sympathies?

He hadn't even been due to attend that function earlier. It had been a last-minute decision, purely because he'd wanted to check on how the hotel was doing.

Everything he'd learned this evening made a kind of sick sense based on how Flora had behaved in his office that day.

*The day you stood her up in public.*

His conscience pricked.

She'd been shocked. Bewildered. And then, stoic when leaving. Not hinting for a second that she was walking out into…nothing.

So, was she really a victim of her uncle too? If so, then Vito had done her a serious injustice.

He left the puppy momentarily to go to Flora's room. The door was ajar and he pushed it open. For a second he couldn't see her but then he made out a shape on the bed and went in further.

She was on top of the covers, in a robe. A towel half on, half off her head. Dark brown and golden curly strands escaping. Her chest was softly rising and falling. One bare leg was exposed. Pale. Long and shapely.

Vito's pulse tripped. He felt like a voyeur. A little

flash of something white and grey and brown streaked past his feet.

*The dog.*

It had obviously followed her smell and was now trying to jump up onto the bed. It was too high.

The dog looked at Vito with huge pleading eyes. Vito cursed and scooped it up and put it on the bed, where it went and curled straight into Flora's side, into a little ball of fluff.

Vito walked back out of the room before she could wake and witness him staring at her as if he'd never seen a woman before.

Flora Gavia was already exposing him in ways he'd never anticipated and, as much as he trusted that this wasn't some elaborate ruse, he definitely wasn't letting her out of his sight until he knew for sure.

# CHAPTER FOUR

WHEN FLORA WOKE she felt as if she was emerging from the deepest and most peaceful sleep she'd ever had. When she opened her eyes she had to squint. It was bright daylight. Her phone was on a nightstand beside the bed and she looked at it and jackknifed up to sitting, the damp towel falling off her head. She groaned. She could only imagine what state her hair was in.

It was lunchtime. Later than she'd ever slept in her life. And she was in Vittorio Vitale's apartment. In his guest room. And where was Benji?

She got up and washed herself and pulled on a pair of faded jeans and a T-shirt. She couldn't do much with her hair so she just pulled it back into a bun.

She left the room and made her way down corridors, eventually emerging into the living room. She saw French doors open and heard an excited yapping. She followed the sound to see a young man in a suit throwing a ball for Benji. The man looked up and went red. She recognised him as the man who'd admitted her to Vittorio's office on the wedding day. 'Miss Gavia, I'm Tommaso, Signore Vitale's assistant. I'll let him know you're up. He's in his home office.'

He'd fled before Flora could say anything and Benji

was running around her feet excitedly. She picked him up and snuggled him close. She frowned then as a half-memory, half-dream returned. Had Benji been on the bed with her last night? And had someone come to take him that morning?

Flora thought of Vittorio coming into the room and seeing her sprawled on the bed in complete disarray and a flush of heat climbed through her body. And of course he chose that moment to appear in front of her, when her face was glowing like a beacon.

He was dressed in black trousers and a light blue shirt, top button open. He said, 'You must be hungry. Let's have lunch. Tommaso will take Benji out for a walk.'

Tommaso appeared again and whisked Benji away. Flora said redundantly, 'Thank you, but I can take him out myself. I don't expect your staff to dog-sit. Anyway, we'll be leaving soon.'

Flora had been following Vittorio into a room off the living room. It was a dining room, through which she could see a kitchen and hear someone whistling. The domestic sound was comforting.

Vittorio pulled out a chair where there was a setting laid out. Flora sat down. Vittorio sat opposite her. He said, 'It's no problem. Tommaso is happy to help. So, where exactly are you planning on going?'

Flora was distracted by Sofia appearing with a light pasta starter that smelled delicious. She looked at Vittorio. 'I'm sorry, what?'

'You said you'll be leaving soon. Where are you planning on going?'

Flora's insides cramped a little. She didn't have anywhere to go. And with a dog in tow that would be even more challenging. She affected an airy tone. 'Oh, we'll find somewhere. I have some contacts.'

'Not many places will take a dog.'

Flora wanted to glare at him. She didn't need to hear her fears articulated back to her. 'I'm sure we'll be fine.' She speared a piece of pasta and put it in her mouth.

'So far you've been on the streets, then in a hostel and then a women's aid centre—your track record hasn't exactly been…stellar.'

Now Flora felt defensive. 'I did the best I could with what little I had. The wedding dress didn't fetch as much as I'd hoped.'

'You sold the dress?'

'It was all I had to sell.'

She saw Vittorio go pale under his tan at the thought of her being driven to drastic measures, and said hurriedly, 'It never came to that. It wouldn't have.'

'It could have,' he said darkly.

'Well, it didn't. I sold the dress for a few hundred euros and that kept me going.'

'It was worth thousands.'

Vittorio had bought the dress. Flora said, 'The second-hand designer wedding-dress market isn't as robust as you might think.'

'You could have made a lot more for the engagement ring, but you left it behind.'

Flora recalled what she'd said to him. 'I'm sorry for saying you had no taste. That wasn't very nice.'

Vittorio pushed his half-finished plate away. He emitted a sound halfway between a bark of laughter and incredulity. '*You're* sorry? I'm the one who sent you out into the streets to fend for yourself.'

Flora squirmed a little. 'You thought I had money.'

'Why didn't you tell me?' Then he made a face and said, 'I wasn't exactly receptive to hearing your side of things.'

'You could say that, yes.'

Sofia came and took the starters away and returned with mains of chicken in a white wine sauce with baby potatoes and salad. Flora tried not to behave like someone who hadn't had a square meal in months, but it was hard.

She forced herself to leave some food on the plate and had to stop herself asking Sofia if she could bag up the leftovers for Benji. As if reading her mind, though, Sofia winked at Flora and said, 'Don't worry, Benji will get some choice pieces of chicken.'

Flora grinned at Sofia. Who would have known she'd find such a sanctuary in Vittorio Vitale's home? She looked at him and he had an arrested expression on his face. She stopped smiling. 'What is it? You keep looking at me as if I've got something on my face.'

He shook his head and cleared his throat. 'The fact is that we both know that you've got nowhere to go.'

Flora sat up straight. 'That's not true, I have lots of…' She trailed off and sagged back a little. She never had been much good at lying.

Sofia brought coffees and biscotti. Flora took a fortifying sip. As the tart strong drink went down her throat she said, 'I'll find something. It's not your concern.'

'Well, I think it is. I feel responsible for letting you go the last time without ensuring your well-being and security. I was distracted and blinded by besting your uncle. I don't like to admit it, but you were peripheral to my agenda with him and this time I'm going to take responsibility for my actions.'

Now Flora was suspicious. 'What's that supposed to mean—take responsibility?'

Vittorio stood up and walked over to the window, hands in his pockets. The action drew the material of his trousers taut over his muscular buttocks. Then he turned around and Flora had to avert her gaze up, guiltily.

'What that means is that I have a proposition.'

Now Flora felt nervous. 'Vittorio—'

'Call me Vito. The only person who called me Vittorio was my mother when she was angry with me.'

Flora's heart squeezed at the mention of his mother. 'Very well… Vito…' she faltered. It felt incredibly intimate calling him Vito. Now she knew why he hadn't invited her to address him as such before, because in his eyes she'd barely existed.

*He'd just apologised for that.*

'What kind of proposition?' And when she said that, why did she feel an illicit flutter of awareness across her skin? This man had no interest in her. Not like that.

'The reason your uncle proposed a marriage arrangement was for his own benefit, of course, but also because he knew the media was speculating about my… social life. My bachelorhood. The fact that it was potentially affecting my business. He saw an opportunity and grabbed it.'

'And then you grabbed it right back,' pointed out Flora. Using her as the unfortunate pawn.

Vito conceded that with a nod of his head. 'But the fact remains that there was some logic in your uncle's plan outside his own nefarious aims. And the situation hasn't changed.'

Flora frowned. 'Meaning…'

'Speculation is still rife as to my…love life. Standing you up at the altar didn't exactly enhance my reputation.'

Flora's heart quickened. 'So you don't…have a girlfriend at the moment?' She winced inwardly. A man like Vito didn't do girlfriends. She recalled seeing a picture of him in the papers shortly after that fateful day—he'd been at an event with one of Italy's most beautiful models. The gossip had been intense. She'd actually been grateful that she wasn't recognisable or else the paparazzi would have had a field day documenting her fall from grace.

Vito was shaking his head. 'No, there's no one in particular.'

A spark of something dark made Flora say, 'Just casual lovers, then.'

Vito's jaw clenched and then he said tightly, 'Actually, not even casual lovers for a while. I haven't had much interest.'

Flora's silly heart skipped again. 'It's none of my business.'

'It will be.'

'How's that?'

'What I propose is that we get back together.'

'But we never were together, not really.'

'True. But that doesn't really matter. If we're seen to be together again, it'll restore your reputation and it'll stop the speculation about my private life.'

'It wasn't much of a secret that our marriage was a

business deal,' she pointed out, still stung by some of the whispers she'd heard from people leaving the church.

*'Of course, he was never going to marry a mouse like her. A man like Vittorio Vitale needs a real woman.'*

It was that comment in particular that had galvanised her to come to his offices to find him. The thought of more humiliation wasn't particularly appealing.

He said, 'So who's to say that it's not something else now? Something more.'

That audacious thought sent an electric charge across her skin. But of course he didn't actually mean it. It was a hypothetical question. Flora shook her head, struggling to understand. 'But why…would you want to do this with me of all people? You hate me.'

Vito shook his head. 'Not you. Your uncle.'

She frowned. 'But won't he benefit from you being seen with me?'

Vito's mouth thinned. 'If anything it'll highlight his exile even more. He wouldn't dare come near me.'

Flora shivered a little. She'd seen what it was like to be on the wrong side of this man.

'I… I'd have to think about it. I've made a bit of a life for myself. I know you might not think it's much, but I have hope for the future, that I can survive. Me and Benji. We just need help getting on our feet.'

'Which is what I'm offering you.'

'What *are* you offering exactly?'

A look came into his eyes that Flora didn't like. It was something between knowing, cynical and weary.

'What do you want?'

Her mind went blank. What she wanted she'd already

got in a way—freedom from her uncle. A life of her own. She was happy to work for her own security.

'What's your price, Flora?'

She looked at him, eyes narrowed. There it was, the world-weary cynicism. She rebelled against it. Even after everything she'd been through, loss, pain, grief, the sterile care of her uncle and aunt, she still retained some sense of hope and a belief in good.

A little rogue inside her urged her to play him at his own game. She lifted her chin. 'I want money, Vito. Isn't that what everyone wants?'

Vito didn't know why he felt so…disappointed. Underneath it all, Flora Gavia was like everyone else, every other woman. She wanted to feather her nest. And he was offering her exactly what she wanted.

Whether or not she'd manipulated him to this exact point, he still wasn't sure and that irritated him. Even now when she was brazenly saying she wanted money.

But then…something about the expression on her face caught him. Her eyes. As if she was mocking him, or… felt sorry for him. Instantly he felt exposed.

'What is it? What are you up to, Flora?'

She stood up. She was slight in her jeans and T-shirt, but he was acutely conscious of her curves under the thin material of her top. The tiny waist he'd noticed on the wedding day. Hips flaring out. The swell of her breasts.

This was a mistake. The woman was a serious irritation and maybe he should just let her and the damn dog—

'You're unbelievable,' she said, cutting through his thoughts. 'You're the most cynical person I ever met. Even worse than my uncle, and that's saying something.'

Vito's face was like stone. 'Everyone has a price, Flora, whether they like to admit it or not.'

Flora was about to deny that but she clamped her mouth shut. Maybe she was being hasty here. Vittorio Vitale was one of the most powerfully wealthy men in the world. There was a lot he could do. Maybe she did have a price.

She looked at him. 'If I did want something…it wouldn't have to be for me, would it?'

He frowned. 'Like what?'

'I don't know…yet.'

Vito shrugged. 'You get to decide what you want to do with it. No strings attached.'

*It* being whatever price she deemed she was worth for Vito to pretend that they were back together? The notion was so ridiculous that she almost felt like laughing. But then she remembered her uncle and aunt, and how every conversation had revolved around money and who had it or didn't.

She remembered that they had plundered her inheritance. All she'd had left of her beloved parents.

Vittorio Vitale was a man from that world. Where everything revolved around money and power and ambition. No wonder it was the only language he knew. He'd been bereaved as a young man and had set out to avenge his parents, accruing great wealth and power along the way.

Motivated by revenge. And yet, since she'd seen him again he'd shown aspects of himself that she never would have expected of the cold and ruthless man who had stood her up on their wedding day. Flora's head was whirling.

'I have to think about all of this... I'm going to go for a walk. I'll find Tommaso and send him back. I'm sure he has more to be doing for you than walking my dog.'

Flora had slipped out of the room before Vito could say anything else. He couldn't really believe that she wasn't negotiating terms. That she wasn't immediately naming a price.

It had been so long since he'd dealt with anyone who didn't look at him as if calculating how much they could get out of him—business colleagues and women—that it was more than a novelty. It was disconcerting. He had nothing to bargain with. And that made him feel a little...redundant.

If he had nothing he could offer Flora then would she even stay? And why did that suddenly matter?

*Because she intrigues you and you want her. You want the woman who you stood up at the altar. You haven't forgotten her in six months.*

This situation was unprecedented. Vito had never had to think much about pursuing a woman he wanted, never intending on a liaison lasting long. Because his main focus had always been on building up his business and taking Umberto Gavia down.

But now, he wanted a woman who came with strings attached. More than strings. A dog. And yet it wasn't making him reconsider. He was too hungry for her.

He'd taken that model out—on the evening of the day he'd been due to marry Flora Gavia. It had been intended as a very clear message to Umberto Gavia and the world that Vito was triumphant.

But that evening and date had been a disaster. He'd been distracted. The model—he couldn't even remember her name—had been uninteresting and not remotely appealing to Vito.

And now, in light of what Flora had been facing when she'd left his office, the memory left a distinctly sour taste in his mouth.

Since that day, Vito had found that the life that he'd been living—high-octane working and socialising—had suddenly felt…a little empty. He'd put it down to the anticlimax of taking over Gavia's business. And so he'd put his head down and used the time to consolidate his position, to make sure that he was invulnerable to any kind of attacks in the future.

But as soon as he'd laid eyes on Flora Gavia again something had pulsed back into life inside him. A desire to engage again. Desire for a woman. Hunger.

The fact that it was *her* of all people was not entirely welcome, but he assured himself that even if she was up to something, he would be prepared. It wasn't as if he wasn't expecting it.

A little voice reminded him that he'd felt something for her on the wedding day, when she'd appeared in that dress. He'd noticed her then. She'd made a mark, a mark that hadn't been made before. Because he hadn't noticed her previously. Or had deliberately chosen not to. Not wanting the distraction.

But now he was distracted. And he was going to do whatever it took to persuade her that he at least owed her sanctuary. As for anything more than that…he'd seen the way she blushed whenever he looked at her. He knew when a woman wanted him. They were both adults. If she was prepared to admit that she felt the same chemistry as him, then perhaps this offer of sanctuary could become something much more mutually satisfying.

He went back into his home office and made some calls. When he heard a light knock on the door, he looked up to see Flora framed in the doorway, the dog in her arms looking pretty content.

Vito could empathise. He stood up. 'Please, come in. Can I get you anything?'

Flora came in and stood on the other side of the desk. She shook her head. Some of her hair had come loose from her bun and was framing her face in curly tendrils.

Once again Vito wondered how on earth he hadn't appreciated her allure until the wedding day, and now.

She put the dog down and he ambled around the room, sniffing. She said, 'I've had a think about your…proposition.'

Vito waited, feeling unexpectedly tense. He really wasn't sure which way this woman would go and usually he read people with ease.

She looked at him. 'I've decided that I'll stay. I'll agree to this plan…to appear as if we are together. It can only help me regain some sort of dignity and respect and give me an opportunity to give something back.'

'Give something back…what do you mean?'

'I'd like you to give a generous donation to the women's aid centre. They need every euro they can get and they need new facilities. I know that's a lot to ask but—'

'Consider it done.'

Flora's eyes widened. 'You mean…you mean that you'll donate, *and* help them get new facilities?'

Vito shrugged. 'I invest in charities all the time, and they're a great cause. They should have been on my radar before now.'

'But it could mean…millions.'

'They need it. You said so yourself.'

'Yes, but I wasn't thinking you'd just agree and offer so much in one fell swoop.'

'Maybe I'm trying to impress you.'

Flora blushed. Vito's body tightened all over.

She said, 'You know you're an impressive guy, but I'm not here to be impressed.'

Vito was struck once again by the way she seemed to be so determined not to take advantage of his interest. To flirt with him.

Curious, he asked, 'What do you want for yourself?'

She shook her head. 'Nothing, really. Oh, no, wait, I'll need help with vet bills for Benji…but I'll pay you back for that when I can.'

'The dog. And the women's aid centre. Nothing for you.'

She looked at him as if he were talking in tongues. 'I've never had anything…so I'm not sure what you mean. My uncle put a roof over my head and hired tutors. I believed that he used my inheritance for that. Now I know he used it for a lot more. But I can't be bitter about it because what's the point? The money is gone. He got his due in the end. I can't say I'm sorry that he is where he is.'

'But what about *your* future?'

Now Flora looked shy. 'I'd like to do some kind of a

course. I've always been interested in design and graphics. I helped the women's aid centre come up with a new logo.'

'I could pay for a course.'

Flora shook her head again. 'I know you could, without even blinking, but my independence is important to me. My whole life was spent feeling obligated to my uncle. He never let me forget that he was taking me in, caring for me—'

'While embezzling you,' Vito pointed out.

'Yes. That too. But if I do a course, I want to pay for it myself. I'll get a job and make my own way. Maybe you could just help with some references or something like that…'

Vito couldn't quite compute this. If Flora was playing a game, it was a very long one. He should know—that was what he'd done with her uncle. But, in his gut, he felt he knew the answer. There was no game here.

For a disconcerting second, Vito felt as if the ground beneath him were shifting. Moving. As if he might have to put out a hand to steady himself. But the only thing within reach was her. And he hadn't had to use anyone to steady himself in a long time. Hadn't needed it.

He pushed a piece of paper and a pen across the desk. 'Write down your contact at the women's aid centre and I'll put my team in touch. They'll set up a meeting and we can ascertain the best way to go about helping them.'

Flora sat down on the chair behind her, almost as if the stuffing were knocked out of her. 'That's really amazing. Thank you.' She wrote down a name and pushed the paper back.

Vito felt something unfamiliar in his chest. A glow.

Warmth. Then a little line furrowed between her brows and she said hesitantly, 'So how would this work exactly? How would we show people that we're…together?'

Flora still felt a little as if the wind had been knocked out of her. She couldn't believe that Vito was agreeing to her request with such speed and generosity. Okay, so he was rich enough to do something like this, but she wasn't used to rich people being generous. Her uncle had been one of the meanest people she'd ever known.

He perched on the edge of the table now and his thigh was in her peripheral vision. She had to fight not to let her gaze drop.

He said, 'We'll go to social events together. Which will mean being photographed together. Which will inevitably draw interest once they realise who you are… but we can spin it that after the wedding was called off, we met again and reconnected and a real relationship grew out of the ashes of the business deal.'

He was *so* cynical. 'You sound like you have it figured out.'

He shrugged lightly. 'We need to be prepared because the press interest will be intense. But I'll make it clear that it has nothing to do with your uncle or mending any bridges.'

Flora felt a small pang for her uncle but then quashed it. He didn't deserve her concern or sympathy. Her own father had moved away from Italy to get away from his brother, not liking his business methods, and the only reason Flora had ended up with him was because her parents obviously hadn't expected that something so tragic as a fatal accident would befall them, and there had been no guardian mentioned in their will. Her uncle had been her only next of kin.

It was only in the last six months that his act of benevolence in taking her in had taken on much darker hues.

She forced her mind back to what Vito was saying. 'So we'd just have to appear together...but won't people know we're not together when they see us? We're not a couple.'

A gleam came into Vito's eye. It made Flora's skin feel suddenly tight and prickly. He said, 'We'll have to make it look like we're a couple.'

'How, exactly?'

Vito stood up and came around the desk. He held out a hand. Flora's heart thumped. She looked at it suspiciously. Vito said, 'It's just a hand, Flora, it won't bite you.'

No, maybe not. But the thought of putting her hand in his suddenly felt like a ridiculously audacious thing to do. She lifted her hand and slipped it into his palm. His fingers closed around hers and he pulled her up to standing.

Since when had he moved so close that their bodies were practically touching? All Flora could smell was him. Musky and woodsy and spicy. Masculine. She wanted to close her eyes and breathe deep. It was an effort not to do that.

She had to look up. He was so much taller than her. He made her feel incredibly petite. Delicate. He was looking at her. His gaze moving over her face, resting on her mouth. It tingled. She had to swallow. Her throat was dry.

'What are you doing?' she asked, trying to break the languor that was spreading through her body.

'I'm showing you how we might have to...touch. Interact. To make people think we're together.'

'Oh.' Flora's brain didn't seem to want to function.

'You see,' Vito was saying, 'I don't think we'll have to pretend all that much.'

'We won't?'

He shook his head. He lifted his other hand and before Flora knew what he was doing, her hair was loosening from its confinement and falling around her shoulders. Vito was looking at her, running the long strands through his fingers. Flora felt as though she wanted to purr.

Then he said, 'The truth is that I don't think either of us will have to pretend.'

She lifted her gaze to his and her heart stopped at the look in his eyes. It was smouldering. This close she could see flecks of gold, like little fires.

*He wanted her.*

It hit her right in her solar plexus, and deep in her core. Between her legs a pulse throbbed, making her press her thighs together as if that could stem the damp, hot reaction.

She knew it was important to try and hang onto some dignity here. It must be so obvious that she fancied him and he was just a very good actor making her believe that he wanted her too because there was no way it could be real.

Vito tipped Flora's chin up and his head lowered. Every part of her quivered with anticipation. And when that firm, sexy mouth touched hers, she knew in that instant she'd never be the same again. He was scorching her alive, from the inside out. She'd never felt anything like it.

His hands moved, cupping her face, holding her so that he could entice her to open up to him, which she did on a helpless sigh. And then the scorching became an inferno when his tongue touched hers.

Flora was lost in a swooning dizzy dance. Time had stopped and all that existed was how it felt to be kissed by this man, her whole body being set alight from between her legs to her breasts.

She didn't even realise she was clutching his arms to remain standing until he pulled back for a moment. Oxygen got to her brain. She opened her eyes. She loosened her death grip on his biceps. Tried to make sense of what had just happened. Vito was watching her, eyes glittering.

There was a sound from the ground. A growling. Flora looked down to see Benji glaring up at Vito. She bent down and scooped him up, as much to do something with her trembling hands as anything else.

She took a step back and eventually said, 'Wow. I mean, yes, okay, I see what you mean. That was…very convincing. If I didn't know better I'd think that you did really want to kiss me. But then I've never been kissed before so I guess I wouldn't really know the difference.'

He frowned. 'I wasn't trying to convince you of anything. I *was* kissing you for real. I do want you, Flora. The electricity between us is off the charts.'

Her belly swooped alarmingly and her legs felt weak. 'I… Okay, that's good, then, isn't it?'

She sneaked a look at Vito. He was frowning. 'Wait a second…you just said you'd never been kissed before… Are you innocent?'

Flora's face burned. Benji was squirming in her arms so she put him down again—the traitor—and stood up.

Of course Vito must have noticed her gauche inexperience, even if she hadn't just admitted it.

There really was nothing to say except to admit the bald truth. 'Yes, I'm a virgin, if that's what you mean.'

# CHAPTER FIVE

VITO LOOKED INCREDULOUS. No doubt virgins were as mythical as unicorns in his very cynical world. He said, 'But…how?'

Now Flora felt self-conscious. She wrapped her arms around herself. A minute ago she'd been melting and now she felt cold. 'I didn't have much of a social life. I was home-schooled. When I graduated, my uncle preferred to keep me at the palazzo, helping him and my aunt to host their parties.'

'You could have left,' Vito pointed out.

Now Flora felt even more vulnerable. 'I could have, yes. But somehow, whenever I contemplated it, my uncle always said something that made me feel like I hadn't paid my dues yet. And when I asked about my inheritance he told me he had it tied up with stocks and shares, trying to make sure I got the most out of it. Then…the marriage deal with you was struck…and for the first time I felt like maybe I finally had a way out. My dues would be paid.'

Vito took a step back. He was shaking his head. 'This changes everything.'

Flora immediately feared for the women's aid home. 'Are you going back on what you promised?'

'No, of course not. But we don't need to appear in public. I won't put you through unnecessary scrutiny.'

Flora struggled to understand. 'But…you just said you wanted me?' She'd never felt as exposed as she did in that moment.

'I do want you, more than I've wanted a woman in a long time.' He sounded grim.

The relief that flooded her was nothing short of humiliating. But she couldn't help asking, 'So…what's the problem?'

Vito's jaw clenched. He said tautly, 'I don't sleep with innocents. I won't be your first lover, Flora. And I wouldn't be able to stand next to you and not touch you. After a kiss like that there's only one way it would end. In my bed.'

A wave of heat pulsed through Flora's body as she thought of where they might be right now, naked limbs entwined, Vito's hands exploring every inch of her flesh—she shook her head, desperately trying to dislodge the images.

She tried to claw back any sense of dignity she could. 'Well, it's very presumptuous of you to imagine that I would have allowed that to happen.'

She wanted to cringe. Who was she kidding? He'd just kissed her and she'd been ready to climb into his skin. She wouldn't have put up a word of protest.

Vito said, 'If you could have resisted, then you would have had more control than me.'

The thought of driving this man so crazy with desire that he wouldn't be able to control himself was heady.

Flora forced herself to parse the information. She asked, 'What is it about my virginity that is so off-putting?'

Vito was pacing again. He stopped and faced her. 'I'm not the man you want as your first lover, Flora. I can't promise anything more than having fun while we both get what we need and want out of this…relationship. You deserve someone who really cares for you. Who'll be gentle.'

Flora felt like growling. There was a fire burning inside her. A fire this man had set alight. The last thing she wanted was gentle, or someone who cared for her. She wanted this man. Only this man. He'd already ruined her and he'd only kissed her!

'I didn't know you held me in such high esteem.' She couldn't help sound mocking.

Vito scowled.

She uncrossed her arms from around herself. 'What if I wasn't a virgin?'

'We wouldn't be having this conversation.'

Flora shivered. They'd be doing something else. 'So what happens now?'

'I'll do what I promised and help the women's aid centre and you're free to stay here until you get a job.'

'What about your precious reputation?'

A muscle in Vito's jaw popped. He said, 'I'll live with it.'

'I'm sure there are any number of women who'd be willing to act the part. Women who aren't virgins. The question is why haven't you just chosen a suitable woman before now? Why me?'

* * *

The truth? Because no other woman had appealed to him enough to even play out a fake relationship for the sake of it. Until Flora. She had inspired the notion. No other woman had made him want to seduce her in a long time. Until Flora.

Except what had happened just now hadn't even been a seduction, it had been blunt and seriously lacking in finesse. But he'd had to kiss her. He'd had to *know*. And now he did and now he couldn't see anything else but her.

But he couldn't have her. He had a rule. He would not sleep with innocents. There was too much of a risk of emotional attachment. And he was not in the market for emotional attachment.

That way lay loss, grief and pain. After losing his parents, Vito had vowed that he would never let anyone close again. And he hadn't. And that wasn't going to change.

He had no desire for a wife, or family. He had no desire to lose everything again. He'd built himself up from the ashes of grief once, he wouldn't be able to do it again.

And while he knew rationally that there was no reason to believe he would suffer such loss again, there was also no guarantee that he wouldn't. And he wasn't prepared to take the risk.

*Coward.*

He had his business and that was all he needed, along with taking his pleasures when and where he could. Restoring the Vitale name and turning it from a byword for shoddy work practices and whispers of corruption into something respected and revered was his life's work. If he could ensure his name became an enduring brand, eclipsing the name Gavia for ever, and if his success benefited others less fortunate, then that was all the legacy he needed.

He said, 'This conversation is over. You're welcome to stay until you're on your feet. But that'll be the extent of our relationship.'

'Flatmates.'

'Essentially.'

Her eyes narrowed on him and, for the first time since he'd met her, Vito saw something that looked suspiciously calculating in those golden-brown depths. But then it was gone.

She bent down and scooped up Benji and said, 'Okay, fine. I'll stay out of your way as much as I can. You'll hardly know I'm here.'

Vito watched Flora leave the room, her wild hair spilling down her back. He wanted to reach out and wrap a lock of that hair around his hand and tug her back and finish what they'd started.

He cursed. What a time to discover that he really did have a conscience.

Later that evening, Vito was back in the apartment after spending the rest of the day in the office. A day where he'd been distracted and irritable. A day where he couldn't stop replaying that kiss in his head. Probably one of the most chaste kisses he'd ever experienced but one that had left him on fire.

And then he'd had to endure an interminably boring business dinner.

He hadn't seen Flora or the dog on his arrival back at the apartment. Sofia was gone for the day. He presumed Flora was in bed. It was late. He imagined her in bed, alone, her hair spread around her head like a halo… He took a healthy swig of his whiskey, hoping the burn would eclipse the other burn.

He was standing at the window, looking out over the view of Rome. It never failed to buoy him up. To remind him of how far he'd come. Restoring his father's legacy and pride in the family name.

*What's it all for, though, if you've no one to leave it to? Is a brand really going to last without someone to protect it?*

He scowled at his reflection and at the insidious doubts infiltrating his head. He was quite happy with his life of no entanglements. And today he'd had the sense to walk away from a potentially explosive one. *Flora.* An innocent.

Just at that moment, he caught a moving flash of silver out of the corner of his eye. He tensed and turned around. 'Flora? Is that you?'

Nothing for a beat and then, from outside in the hall, 'Um, yes, it's me.'

'What are you doing?'

'Going out.'

Vito frowned and put the glass down on a table. He walked to the door and looked into the corridor that led to the reception hall and almost choked at what he saw. Flora, but not Flora. A different woman. His brain was melting and his entire body was going up in flames.

Somehow he managed to croak out, 'What are you wearing?'

Flora was trembling all over but refused to let Vito's reaction put her off. She knew the dress was audacious.

It was why she was wearing it. It had been a hand-me-down from one of the women at the shelter, along with the matching four-inch stilettos that she could barely walk in. The woman had said, 'Take it—with your figure it'll look amazing.' Flora had taken it, as much out of politeness as anything else.

But this evening she'd realised it was perfect for what she needed.

*To get rid of her virginity.*

If she couldn't do it in this dress, then she might as well take a vow of chastity. Vito had laid down a gauntlet earlier. Even if he didn't know it. Flora had realised that she didn't want her innocence to hold her back. She had no great romantic illusions after growing up in a loveless environment. This was a very practical decision. She wanted Vito, therefore she needed to remove the impediment: her virginity.

She said, 'I'm wearing a dress.' But even as she said that she winced. It was just a scrap of material really. Thin straps and a low V-neck, with hundreds of little silver medallions stitched into the fabric that moved and shimmered with every breath she took. She couldn't wear a bra with the dress so she felt very conscious of her breasts under the thin material.

It fell to her upper thigh, just about scraping the edges of decency.

Vito's eyes were almost bugging out of his head. He said, 'That's not a dress, that's an invitation to sin.'

His reaction galvanised Flora. 'Good, I was hoping for that effect.'

His gaze moved up to meet hers. 'Why?'

'Because if my virginity is such an impediment I intend to get rid of it. If you won't be my first lover, then I'll find someone who will. You made me realise today that I don't want my innocence holding me back.'

She turned around to leave and prayed that she wouldn't humiliate herself by falling flat on her face in these ridiculous shoes.

Vito said from behind her, 'Where are you going?'

Without turning around, she said, 'I'm going to Diablo. I hear it's the best nightclub in town.'

'Do you know how much it costs to get in?'

Aiming for more confidence than she felt and going off what she'd heard about the club—that if they deemed you alluring enough they would let you in for free—Flora said, 'I don't think it'll be an issue, do you?' She really hoped it wouldn't be. She was counting on this dress being enough of a distraction to get her in.

'That place is full of sharks.'

Flora was in the entrance hall now and she turned around. 'You'd know, I guess.' She didn't mean it as an insult, merely as a fact.

Vito's face was stony. But he said, 'Something like that.'

Then he shook his head and came towards her. Flora stood her ground. He said, 'You won't find the kind of man you want in a place like that, Flora.'

'You don't know what kind of man I want.'

*I want you.*

She turned around again and was almost at the private elevator doors when Vito said from behind her, 'This is crazy.'

She pressed the button and the doors opened. He said, 'You wouldn't dare.'

She just said, 'Watch me,' and stepped into the elevator.

# CHAPTER SIX

VITO ENTERED THE dark decadent space, lit up by strobing lights. The thumping bass of the music reached all the way down to his bones, but he noticed none of it. He was looking for a wild-haired temptress in a glittering excuse for a dress.

'Vito, man! Where the hell have you been?'

Vito ignored the greeting.

He got to the other side of the bar where he stood at a railing. The dance floor was below and thick with people, their sinuous bodies moving in time with the music. Heads thrown back, arms around necks, bodies pressed together. It was temptation and sin and decadence and he wondered what he'd ever seen in it. It all seemed a little desperate and tacky to him now.

Full of predators.

*Like you.*

Vito made a face, scaring off one woman who had been approaching him.

And then, a flash of silver caught his eye and he saw her. She was on the edge of the dance floor, surrounded by a group of men. Of course she'd got in. He couldn't imagine a bouncer in the world denying her entry. She was holding a delicate flute of sparkling wine.

She laughed at something one of the men said but Vito could see that she didn't look entirely comfortable. They were hemming her in.

Then she looked up and over their heads, straight at him. She lifted her glass in a salute and then downed the drink in one, handing her empty glass to one man while taking another by the hand and leading him onto the dance floor.

The man looked as if all his Christmases had just come at once. Vito was going to kill him. He refrained from vaulting over the rail onto the dance floor and took the stairs.

His blood was pounding along with the music, but with one refrain, *Mine, mine, mine.* He had forgotten all about his conscience. The minute he'd seen Flora in that dress his conscience had turned to dust.

She was his and he was going to have her, over and over, until he could breathe again.

Flora was feeling a little dizzy after downing that drink in one go. A little reckless, but when she'd seen Vito standing at the railing scouring the crowd for her, she'd wanted to taunt him.

She was done with men trying to keep her in a box. First her uncle's palazzo and now Vito's plush apartment. She wanted to live. She wanted to be devoured. The only problem was that the only man she wanted to devour her was more likely to drag her out of here and scold her than devour her.

The man she had pulled onto the dance floor was now dancing energetically opposite her, his avid gaze firmly fixed on her breasts. She smiled weakly. This wasn't panning out exactly as she'd hoped. It felt a bit tawdry.

But suddenly he was gone and in his place was a man about a foot taller, and broader and altogether more dynamic. *Vito.*

She stopped moving and looked up. And gulped. His gaze was on fire. His face was stark. Jaw clenched. Flora put her hands on her hips. 'I'm not leaving.'

'Yes, you are.'

'No, I'm not. I'm having sex tonight and if you don't want it to be with you then please get out of my way.'

'You will not be having sex tonight with anyone *but* me,' Vito breathed.

The music was almost deafening but Flora heard that as clear as a bell. Her heart thumped. 'What did you say?'

He reached for her and put his hands on her waist. He tugged her closer until their bodies were touching. She could feel the ridge of his arousal. Her heart rate went up to a million beats a minute. He was still wearing his work clothes, white shirt and dark trousers. He should have looked ridiculous. He was the sexiest man there.

He said succinctly, 'You heard me.'

She had heard him but she didn't quite believe him. Maybe he was just trying to get her out of this den of iniquity.

'What are you saying exactly, Vito?'

Vito moved his hands around to her back, hauling her closer. His hands were on her bare skin. She was throbbing. And down between her legs, she was damp.

He said, 'I want you, Flora.'

'But you didn't want to be my first lover.'

'Let's just say I've reconsidered.'

Flora could see the day-old stubble on his jaw darkening it, making it look even harder. She reached up and touched him there, feeling the short bristles, imagining how it would feel on her skin.

He took her hand and pressed his mouth to her inner palm, darting out his tongue. Flora's legs nearly gave way. Vito held her up. He took her hand and said, 'Come on, we're leaving.'

He started to pull her off the dance floor and Flora's insides were somersaulting. At the last second, though, she stalled and he looked back at her, impatience stamped all over his face.

*For her.*

She said, 'Can we just…stay for one more song? I've never been to a nightclub before.'

Vito looked at her and something flickered over his face—surprise. But then he nodded. 'One song.'

Flora tugged him back onto the dance floor, the beat of the music in time with the pounding of her pulse. For the first time in her life, as she danced—inelegantly, she was sure—in front of a man who was looking at her as if she were the only thing on the planet, she felt young and free. Vibrant. Alive. *Seen.* That revelation made her stumble a little. Vito caught her. She didn't want to think about that too closely, how it felt to be seen for herself and not as someone who was just tolerated. It made her feel emotional, and she didn't want to delve into emotions. She wanted the physicality that Vito was offering.

She looked up at him and said, 'Okay, I'm ready to go.'

The journey back to Vito's apartment was made in silence. Once again he drove with a quiet confidence that impressed Flora. Even more so when she thought of those hands and what they would shortly be doing to *her*.

Her whole body felt as if it were vibrating. Maybe the after-effects of the club and the music but more likely the effects of Vito's hands on her. His eyes.

She sneaked a look at his profile as he pulled to a stop outside the building and the concierge came out to park the car. His face was still set in those stark lines. She felt a prickle of unease. 'Vito, if you've changed your mind—'

He looked at her and she stopped talking. He said, 'I've never been more sure of anything in my life.'

Flora licked dry lips. 'What's that exactly?' Because if he was about to say that he wasn't going to do this then she was jumping straight into a cab and going back to the club.

'You and me. I am the only first lover you will know, Flora. You're mine.'

A thrill so electric went through her at his possessive declaration that she quivered with it. 'I… Okay.'

He got out of the car and tossed the keys to the concierge, and came around to help her out. He kept hold of her hand, leading her into the building, to the elevator. The doors closed. Flora took the opportunity to slip out of the shoes, picking them up with her free hand. She muttered, 'I don't know how women wear these all the time.'

The elevator doors opened and before Flora could take another breath, Vito had taken her shoes, thrown them aside and she had her back against the wall beside the elevator doors and his hands were either side of her head.

The air sizzled. Or maybe she was just sizzling.

He said, 'If this evening's stunt was designed to make me change my mind, it worked.'

Flora frowned. It was hard to concentrate when he was so close. *Had* she set out to drive him to pursue her? All she could remember thinking was that if she wasn't a virgin then they could make love.

'I…hadn't really thought it through in such detail. I just wanted to get rid of it so that I could…maybe we could…you know…'

'Make love?'

Flora nodded, relieved that he understood. She looked at his mouth. 'Can we stop talking now?'

He answered that by putting his mouth on hers and she melted into him, hands fisting his shirt to stay standing. His hands were on her face, in her hair and then on her back, fingers spread over her skin.

She ached between her legs. A physical pain to have him touch her there, but he drew back and said harshly, 'Not here, like this.'

He scooped her up into his arms and carried her down the corridor into his bedroom. Flora lifted her head and said, 'Wait! Benji.'

Vito didn't break his stride. 'Taken care of. I asked Damiano to keep him in the security room tonight. We'll get him in the morning.'

*We.* Flora's heart turned over. He hadn't just forgotten about the dog. And now they were truly alone. No interruptions. Vito was going to be her first lover. And she already knew that his mark on her would be indelible. Perhaps fatal. But she didn't care about that now. She was hungry. Starving. For something she'd never known could exist. Desire. No, lust.

She'd always imagined wanting to have sex with someone would feel a little tepid. But this was like a storm, building and building deep inside, threatening to blow her apart.

Vito put her on her feet. She suddenly felt self-conscious. Very aware that she would be joining a legion of women before her and that inevitably she wouldn't stack up next to them.

But Vito was looking at her as if he'd never seen a woman before and Flora clung onto that illusion. He said, 'I want to see you.'

Flora quivered inwardly. No way was she baring herself while suddenly feeling so vulnerable. 'You first.'

Vito didn't hesitate. His shirt came off and Flora barely had time to ogle at the hard-muscled perfection of his chest before he was undoing his trousers and pulling them down, kicking them off.

Now he wore just briefs that did little to hide the bulge. Flora watched wide-eyed, fascinated, as he tugged them down and off too, freeing his impressive erection.

Flora's insides squeezed tight. Then she realised she was squeezing her thighs together as if that could stem the flow of damp heat. Of sheer lust.

Without even making the conscious decision, she reached out and touched Vito's chest. His skin was warm and firm. Dark hairs dusting his pectoral muscles. A line of hair dissected his abdomen and went all the way down to the thicket of hair between his legs.

Hard, powerful thighs. Slim waist. He was intimidatingly perfect. She dragged her gaze back up. She was filled with a sense of their disparities in everything—but mostly experience. 'Vito… I don't know if this is such a good idea. I'm not…experienced, as you know…you're bound to be disappointed…'

He put a finger over her lips. Then he took it away and said, 'Do you want to do this?'

Flora couldn't help but nod. 'More than anything.'

'Then let me see you.'

Flora's heart thumped. She brought a hand to one strap of the dress and pushed it down over her shoulder. Then the other. The dress lowered and clung for a second to her chest.

Vito reached out and, with a flick of his hand, the dress fell under its own weight, all the way to the floor, leaving Flora standing before him wearing nothing but her underwear.

She heard Vito's sharp intake of breath. She was too scared to look at him, see his reaction. There was a stillness in the air. Eventually, he breathed, 'You are…more beautiful than anything I imagined.'

She looked up. He'd imagined this? His eyes were so dark she couldn't read them. He closed the distance between them and cupped her breasts, testing their weight and shape, thumbs moving back and forth over hard nipples.

Flora bit her lip. And then Vito was dipping, capturing her mouth with his again, angling her face up to him so that he could plunder deep. She wrapped her arms around him, opening up her body to his. There was no point where they didn't touch, breast to chest and hips to belly and thighs. It was intoxicating.

Flora felt weightless for a moment and then she realised that Vito was putting her down on the bed. She was dizzy, with desire. He drew back. A lock of hair fell onto his forehead and she reached up and touched it. It made him seem younger, carefree.

He took her hand and captured it, pressing his mouth to her palm again. Tasting her. Need was like a taut wire inside Flora. She said, 'Vito, please… I need you.'

He looked at her. 'I want to make sure you're ready. Your first time might hurt a little.'

She shimmied out of her underwear, throwing the slip of material aside. 'I'll be fine. I'm not made of glass.'

'No,' he breathed, his eyes moving down over her body. 'You're not, are you?'

Still, he didn't move fast. He put his hand on her, between her legs. Flora opened for him, trusting him implicitly. He explored her with a finger, then two, seeking where she ached, finding where she was so hot and wet. Moving in and out, making her hips circle and her head go back.

Then he was thrusting deep, massaging her inner mucles, and Flora was helpless to stop a wave of pleasure breaking her apart. She couldn't breathe for a long moment, absorbing the magnitude of what had just happened.

When she lifted her head, she saw Vito rolling a sheath onto his erection, and then he positioned himself between her legs, holding the full weight of his body off hers.

Even as the last flutters of orgasm were still pulsing through her body, Flora was hungry for more. She tilted her hips towards Vito. He smiled and said, 'Patience, little one.'

She wanted to scowl but then he was nudging the head of his erection against her body and she sucked in a breath when he breached her entrance. He kept going, watching her reaction, inch by inch, until she felt so full that she couldn't breathe, but then she did take a breath, and another, and Vito pulled back out, before moving in again and starting up a rhythm as old as humanity.

Flora was no longer human as she was swept up into a vortex of building pleasure—so intense it almost bordered on being painful. She wrapped her legs around Vito's waist and he sank even deeper, emitting a curse that would have made her smile if she hadn't been so focused on reaching the pinnacle shimmering just out of reach.

But then Vito lowered his head to her breast and took a nipple into his mouth, sucking deep, biting gently and the peak broke over Flora with no warning, making her cry out, her back arch, and every muscle in her body clench tight. She was barely aware of Vito's own guttural cry as his big body jerked against hers, both of them falling over the edge and down into an ocean of endless pleasure.

Dawn was lightening the Rome sky outside but Vito was hardly aware. He was standing, with a towel slung around his hips, a few feet from the bed. He'd just taken a shower and was already lamenting washing Flora's scent from his skin. That made him nervous. This whole situation made him nervous.

He didn't do this. He didn't take women in off the street. He didn't sleep with virgins. He didn't watch lovers as they slept.

But…she was a vision. On her front, one arm raised. The plump flesh of her breast visible. Enticing. Wild hair spread out around her head, reminding him of how he'd wrapped it in his hand as he'd thrust into her over and over again and had chased a pinnacle of pleasure he'd never reached before.

*That's because she was innocent.*

No. It had been more than that. Vito already knew that what had happened last night would only get better. He felt it deep inside. There was something unprecedented about their chemistry.

Making love for him had always been pleasurable but not…transcendent.

A sense of panic clutched at his gut. A sense of claustrophobia. But then he forced it back down. Reminding himself of all that he'd been through. All that he'd mastered. A woman couldn't undo that, no matter how amazing the sex. And that was all it was. Amazing sex. He wanted to bark out a laugh at himself, for almost losing it. Over a woman. Over sex.

Vito was a loner. He had no intentions of that changing. He would never suffer the awful excoriating pain of loss and grief again.

But first, he had to set some boundaries and make sure Flora knew that, outside sex, there would be no intimacies. He would take her back to her own room. He didn't indulge women in his bed after sex.

He bent down over the bed, intending to scoop Flora up, but she opened her eyes and saw him. Vito was instantly distracted when that gold-and-brown gaze widened on him.

She moved, and came up on one arm, her breasts swaying with the movement, causing his body to tighten as desire surged.

She looked deliciously sleepy, and well loved. *Sexy.*

He would move her in a minute, but first, 'How are you feeling?'

She frowned, as if gauging, and then with a slow, shy smile, she said, 'I feel good…amazing.' She looked at him. 'I wasn't sure for a second…if it wasn't a dream. But you're not a dream, are you?'

She reached out and touched his clean-shaven jaw with a light touch, but it seared Vito all the way to his gut.

She said, 'You're real. What happened…was real.'

Vito, quite against his intention to scoop her up and take her back to her own bed, found himself flicking off his towel and climbing back onto the bed beside Flora, breathing in her scent and revelling in the way her body curved against his.

His blood was already pounding, hunger clawing. Why on earth would he take her back to her own bed when she was here now, *his*, for the taking? He asked, 'Are you sore?'

She went a little pink. 'Just a bit tender…but I want you again, Vito… Is that too much? Too forward?' She buried her head against him as if she was embarrassed and Vito felt something disturbingly close to an emotion fill his chest. He pushed it back down.

*It was just amazing sex.*

He tipped her chin back up and looked at her. 'No, it's not too much at all. I want you too. But this time…we're going to take it slow…'

He heard the hitch in her breath as his hand moved over her belly and down, exploring her tender flesh and bringing them both back to an urgency that didn't remain slow for very long.

# CHAPTER SEVEN

WHEN FLORA WOKE it was bright daylight outside. She looked at her watch and jackknifed up to sitting. Lunchtime. Again. She'd never been so slovenly in her life.

And then she went still as several things registered. She wasn't in her own room. She was in a very rumpled bed. *Vito's bed.* She was naked. And she had a delicious feeling of languor running through her veins. As if she wanted to just lie back down and luxuriate in the feeling of having been so thoroughly…loved.

A little shiver went through her. It wasn't love. It was just sex. Amazing sex. She'd never known it could be like that. So…all-encompassing. So transformative. She did feel transformed. As if her cells had been realigned and now she was a different verison of herself. *A woman.* Who had awoken to her sensuality.

But the thing that loomed largest in her head now was how considerate and gentle Vito had been. *And not gentle.* But that had been because she'd been urging him on, to stop taking such care.

Heat filled her face now as she remembered how at one point she'd bitten his shoulder. She'd bitten him. Like a mad thing. She buried her face in her hands and cringed.

'What's wrong? Are you hurt? Sore?'

A small bundle of fur landed beside Flora on the bed at the same time as she heard the voice. Benji. Her dog, who she was neglecting terribly, expecting everyone to take on her responsibility.

And Vito, standing in the doorway, dressed in dark trousers and a short-sleeved polo shirt, looking as if he'd just stepped out of *Vogue Italia* for men. She pulled the sheet up over her chest and drew her knees up, while scooping Benji up against her chest, like a shield. He licked her face.

She felt vulnerable and prickly. 'You should have woken me. I should've been up, walking Benji and—' She stopped.

Vito raised a brow. 'And what? You don't have anything to do. Relax.'

Before her life had imploded on that fateful wedding day she'd been busy running the palazzo for her uncle and aunt. And in the last six months she'd been in survival mode. She felt redundant. 'I need to get a job.'

'And I'm sure you will…but after last night I think we're back to Plan A.'

'Which is?'

'Pretending we're back together. I don't think the PDA will be an issue now, do you?'

Flora wanted to scowl at his arrogant self-assurance even though she'd been the one who had all but seduced him!

'I…yes, I guess so.' She couldn't very well say no, now, could she?

Vito glanced at his watch. 'Sofia has prepared some brunch for you and then the glam team will be arriving.'

'The glam team?'

Vito looked at her. 'A stylist and her team of hair and make-up staff. We'll be attending our first function this evening.'

'This evening!' Flora squeaked.

Vito looked at her. 'You've been to social events before.'

Flora shook her head. 'Not really, not outside my uncle's palazzo. He didn't really approve of me attending events that weren't hosted by him.'

Vito was silent for a long moment. 'Did he ever let you out of that palazzo?'

Flora said, 'Of course, I was free to come and go. I'd go to the market with the housekeeper. Or when they were away that's when I'd go out to museums and art galleries.'

'You didn't meet with friends? Go to parties?'

Flora felt self-conscious. 'Not really.' *Never.* She confided reluctantly, 'I had no friends. Like I told you, I was home-schooled.'

Vito came into the bedroom. 'Have you ever left Italy?'

Flora shook her head. 'No. Not since I came here from London after my parents and younger brother, Charlie, died.'

Vito's eyes widened. A look of pure disgust came over his face. 'That man kept you locked up like Cinderella. All you were missing was two evil stepsisters.'

Flora found it hard to breathe for a moment. She'd never had anyone else evaluate the life she'd taken for granted before. And the loyalty and obligation she'd felt to her uncle was still there, like a scar.

'I can't really complain. I had a roof over my head—I lived in a beautiful palazzo. I got my education.'

Vito made a rude sound. 'That palazzo was like something out of a nineteen-fifties film set, straight out of the Cinecittà movie studios.'

A surprised laugh at Vito's accurate assessment came out of Flora before she could stop it. She put her hand over her mouth.

But still, the impulse to be loyal made her say, 'I think my uncle just appreciated another era.'

Vito snorted. 'He appreciated not spending money on anything but creating misery, more to the point.'

Flora sobered. Vito was right. She'd always known her uncle kept her all but locked up, but she'd convinced herself it had been for her protection and security. Now she could understand that he'd done it so that she wouldn't leave before he could get his hands on her inheritance.

The sense of years spent locked out of the world suddenly made her appreciate what was happening here now with Vito. She was being awoken in more ways than one. She felt a sense of urgency. 'What time is the glam team coming?'

'Three o'clock.'

'And what time do you have to go to the office?'

'About half an hour ago.'

Flora summoned up all of her courage and threw back the cover and stood up from the bed. Naked.

'Well, then,' she said, 'as you're already late, what does another half-hour matter?'

Vito's face flushed and his eyes narrowed on her body. For a moment she imagined Vito leaving her standing there, walking away, but then he scooped up Benji, who had trotted over to smell his feet, efficiently put the dog out of the room, closed the door and stalked towards Flora, shedding clothes as he did.

By the time he reached her he was naked. His body gleamed in the sunlight flooding into the room and Flora took her opportunity to really look at him, marvelling at his sheer perfection.

'Keep looking at me like that and we'll be here until tomorrow.' Vito growled, reaching for her, and placing his hands on her waist. She was pressed up against him and she quivered all over at the contact. His erection pressing against her lower belly.

Breathless, she looked up and said, 'And that'd be a bad thing because…?'

Vito took a skein of her hair and wrapped it around his hand. He said, 'Because I have every intention of showing you off this evening and making sure everyone can see the jewel that has been locked away for too long.'

Emotion caught at Flora before she could stop it. Making her chest tight. In a bid to defuse it and distract Vito from just how seismic his words were to her, Flora reached up and wrapped her arms around his neck and then they were falling back onto the bed in a tangle of limbs and sighs and murmurs that grew more frantic and desperate as they lost themselves in each other again.

Flora was looking at herself suspiciously in the mirror. Even Benji was looking at her suspiciously. With his one good eye. Flora said reproachfully to his reflection in the mirror, where he was sitting on the bed behind her, 'It *is* still me, Ben.'

She sniffed her wrist where the stylist had instructed

her to spray some perfume. It was heady—musky rose and something lighter. She liked it even if it didn't feel remotely like her. Maybe it was the scent putting him off.

Because visually, she was almost unrecognisable. Flora had never had a fantasy of being transformed like Cinderella, but if she had…she was living it right now.

The stylist and her team had just left and finally Flora was able to take in the magnitude of what they'd been working on all afternoon. She blushed, thinking of how when she and Vito had emerged from the bedroom after a couple of hours indulging in exploring each other with a thoroughness that had left Flora limp with an overload of pleasure—the glam team had been waiting for her.

Flora had felt like a naughty child caught playing truant. Vito had left her in the hands of the team, but not before she'd heard him instructing the stylist, 'Under no circumstances is her hair to be straightened.' That had caused another rush of emotion to Flora's chest, making her feel as if a layer of skin had been removed, exposing vulnerabilities she'd pushed down for a long time.

But then Vito had left and she'd been sucked into a whirlwind of having her hair trimmed and styled, nails manicured, a facial, her entire body measured to within an inch of its life, all leading to this…vision in the mirror.

The dress was a very pale pink blush colour, strapless and cut across her chest to reveal more cleavage than Flora was comfortable with, but the stylist had assured her it was not too revealing. The bodice was tight and then from her waist the dress fell to the floor in whimsical layers of silk and chiffon.

It was deceptively simple and Flora could barely feel it when she moved. As if it were made of air.

She wore a simple diamond choker and a diamond cocktail ring on her index finger. Diamond stud earrings.

Her hair had been styled in such a way that it was still natural but a little more tamed. The hairdresser had left her some products, telling her they would work miracles. It had been pulled back on one side and held in place with a diamond clip and then teased to flow over the other bare shoulder.

Her make-up was minimal, much to Flora's relief. Or, to be more accurate, she'd been made up to look as if she were wearing very little. Some dusky shimmery blush colour on her eyes, lashes long and black. Eyebrows plucked and shaped. Blush on her cheeks. Her mouth looked plumper—as if she'd just been kissed. She was tempted to find a tissue to make it look less…provocative but then she heard a sound coming from the doorway and turned around.

*Vito.*

Flora instantly forgot her preoccupation with herself. Vito was wearing a tuxedo. She'd seen him in a tuxedo just a couple of nights ago but that had been unexpected and she'd been too distracted to really appreciate the full effect.

But now he was in front of her and she was going to be going out with him and pretending that they were together as a couple…suddenly it was all a bit overwhelming.

Vito frowned. 'What is it? You've gone white.' He was beside her and guiding her to a stool nearby, making her sit down before she could protest. In truth her legs had turned to jelly. The impact of him in the tuxedo, what had happened between them in the last twenty-four hours, added to the sense of overwhelm.

Flora struggled to get air to her brain. Her heart. Vito smelled delicious, which only scrambled her brain cells even more.

Vito handed her a glass of water. Flora took a gulp. She handed it back. Looked up. 'I don't know if I can do this.'

Vito was putting the glass down. 'Do what?'

'Go out with you.' She shook her head. 'I know people think that I come from this very privileged background, but *you* know that's not the case. I've never really been to a society event. That's one of the reasons why there were so many people at the wedding that day, because most of them just wanted to gawk at me.'

Vito's jaw clenched. 'Flora, if I'd thought for a second about how that day was really going to impact you—'

She waved a hand. 'It's not your fault. How could you have known?'

Vito took a step back and held out a hand. 'Come here.'

Reluctantly Flora put her hand in his and let him pull her up. He put his hands on her shoulders and she felt the zing of electricity all the way to between her legs. Her body was like a finely tuned instrument around this man. She could only hope that he felt a smidgeon of what she was feeling but it was unlikely, he was so much more experienced.

He turned her to face the mirror. 'Look at yourself.'

Flora resisted telling him that was exactly what she'd just been doing and what had led to this minor attack of nerves. She looked at him. The first thing she noticed was how tall he was behind her. And his hands, on her shoulders. His skin so much darker than hers.

'Not at me,' he scolded. 'At you.'

Flora rolled her eyes but then did as he asked. He pulled her back against him and she could feel his chest rumble against her back when he spoke. 'You are beautiful, Flora. And I'm ashamed to admit that I was so blinded by your uncle that I didn't notice it properly until you arrived in my office the day of the wedding.'

Flora's gaze met his. Her heart flipped. She felt shy now. 'I noticed you…as soon as I saw you.'

'When you were hiding in the shadows.'

That impacted Flora in a very deep place where she harboured her worst fears and insecurities. 'You were very intimidating.'

'If I had not been so consumed with revenge, I would have noticed you more and maybe things would have been…different.'

Flora gave a little snort. 'You still wouldn't have married me.'

'No, of course not. I'm never getting married. But maybe…we would have realised this mutual desire a lot earlier.'

Flora shook her head and stepped out from under his hands, facing him. 'No, you hated him too much to be associated with anyone close to him.'

Vito looked at her broodingly. 'Perhaps.'

'Anyway,' Flora said, 'I'm glad things worked out the way they did. All ties were finally cut with my uncle and I found my freedom and independence, and I'm never giving it up for anyone again.'

*But you'd consider it for this man.*

That revelation gave her a jolt. On no planet was it likely that she and this man would be anything more than a fleeting interlude. For whatever reason he fancied her right now, but she was sure it wouldn't last long and he wouldn't keep indulging her like this. His guilt would be assuaged and he'd be moving on to the next woman.

And that was okay. Flora wasn't even sure where she really saw herself, or what she wanted long-term. Her uncle had kept her so confined that she was just enjoying her independence and feeling young and free.

*And enjoying Vito*, a little devil prompted.

Vito looked at her and saw the heat coming into her face before she could stop it. He said approvingly, 'That's good, you've got a little colour again.'

Terrified he'd see just how much that was down to him, Flora said, 'We should probably go?'

Thankfully Vito didn't argue or say anything else. He led her out of the room and Flora made sure to install Benji in the kitchen area with his bed and treats, before they went down to the ground level where his driver was waiting.

In the car, as it moved through the traffic, Flora thought of the way Vito had so summarily declared he wasn't going to have a family. She turned to him. 'If you really have no intention of marrying or having a family, then what's all this for, if not to leave a legacy to pass down?' She put out a hand to encompass the city beyond the car.

Vito shook his head, supremely unconcerned. 'I don't need a family to leave a legacy. I lost the only family I ever had and I have no intention of living my life in fear that it'll disappear again. My father's name will endure, I've made sure of that.'

Flora's heart squeezed. She could understand that sentiment, after losing her own family. But she got distracted from pursuing that line of conversation when she saw where they were going. One of Rome's most iconic buildings that housed a venerated museum. It was hosting an event that evening to celebrate a new exhibition with all proceeds from the VIP guest tickets going to charities.

She saw the glittering crowd entering the building, and the sense of panic and overwhelm came back with a vengeance. She couldn't see one woman with her hair down. They were all wearing complicated up-dos and their hair was sleek and shiny.

Flora gripped Vito's hand. 'My hair, Vito, it's too untidy. We should have put it up.'

He looked at her and his mouth quirked. 'Nonsense, you'll be a sensation.'

Flora felt queasy. She didn't want to be a sensation, she wanted to just slip into the crowd and not be noticed and then leave again. But now the car was stopping and Vito was getting out, straightening his jacket and coming around to open her door and putting out a hand. Too late to turn back. She'd set this chain of events in motion when she'd tried to sneak out of his apartment last night looking to find someone to relieve her of her innocence.

And she hadn't failed. Her skin got hot at the memory of what had happened. She'd had a driving force to be with this man in spite of any obstacles like her virginity, and so now she had to fulfil her part in this arrangement.

Flora let Vito pull her out of the car. Her dress fell around her legs in soft folds. She took a deep breath.

'Ready?'

She nodded, mentally steeling herself for the experience.

What she was unprepared for were the photographers lined up along the red-carpeted steps, calling out, *'Vito! Over here! Who is your date, please?'*

They didn't recognise her. The same photographers who had been outside the church waiting for her to emerge after the humiliation of being stood up didn't recognise her. On that wedding day the priest had been kind enough to let her out of a back entrance where he'd had one of the church staff in a car waiting for her.

Her uncle and aunt had just cast her off. She'd had nowhere to go…and in that moment she'd been so angry and humiliated that she'd directed the driver to take her to the only place she could think of. Vito's office. She hadn't even known if he'd be there, but he had been. As if it were a normal working day. Adding insult to injury.

*'Vito, who's your date?'*

Vito squeezed Flora's hand before saying, 'Don't you recognise Flora Gavia?'

There was a moment of almost comically hushed silence and then it was pandemonium with shouting and flashing lights, but Vito managed to get them to the top of the steps and into the foyer of the museum before Flora could absorb the enormity of what had just happened. Vittorio Vitale declaring publicly that he was back with his jilted bride-to-be.

She looked around. Guests were being funnelled up a wide central marble staircase. She'd been to this museum when it was open during the day. Not at night, like this, when it had been transformed. A massive crystal chandelier was overhead, emitting a golden light. Flowers adorned every space, and all along either side of the staircase, sending out heady scents.

The medieval frescoes on the ceiling almost paled in comparison. Flora was so busy looking up that she collided into Vito's back when he stopped. He looked at her and she mumbled, 'Sorry.'

They were on the first level now and being directed into a massive ballroom, or, as Flora knew it, one of the museum's vast rooms, usually stuffed with artefacts from ancient Roman times. That had all been cleared out and now this room was full of Rome's high society being served by waiters wearing black and white. Much as Flora had been doing, not so long ago.

Vito took two glasses of champagne from a tray and handed her one. She took a sip, wrinkling her nose at the bubbles. Golden lighting imbued everyone and everything with a kind of celestial glow. French doors were open onto a wide terrace, which she knew overlooked beautiful landscaped gardens.

'You've been here before?' Vito asked her.

'Of course…with my tutor for schoolwork. Not like this. Although,' she amended then, 'when I was older, finished with schoolwork, I loved coming to the gardens. There's a cafe and you can sit for hours watching people come and go.'

'I'm surprised your uncle gave you the freedom to do that.' Vito's tone was dry.

'Well, he didn't. I did it when they were away on business or travelling.' Flora felt self-conscious now. 'You must think I was very weak to let him have such a hold over me.'

Flora sneaked a look at Vito but he was shaking his head. 'Not at all. I think it must have taken immense courage and fortitude to withstand that hostile environment and emerge with such a forgiving nature.'

Flora felt a glow inside her. But before she could respond to Vito's comment, they were being interrupted by what turned into a long line of people vying for Vito's attention, and all sending Flora more than curious glances.

She heard someone say nearby in a loud whisper, *'Is it really her? I don't think so...she wasn't that pretty.'*

Vito must have heard it too because he wrapped an arm around Flora's waist and turned to face the person behind the whisper. Two women, whose faces went pink. Vito said cordially to one of them, 'Ah, Contessa, I do believe you must know Flora Gavia?'

The woman smiled but it wasn't friendly. She didn't like being caught out. She put out a hand. 'Of course, Miss Gavia, how nice. I dined at your uncle's palazzo many times. How is he?'

Flora took her hand and shook it firmly and said with a bright smile, 'I have no idea. I'm sure that, wherever he is, he's up to no good.'

She heard a stifled snort next to her but didn't look at Vito. When he'd recovered himself he said, 'If you'll excuse us, Contessa?' and he smoothly guided Flora away and they went out onto the terrace.

When they were outside he let out a proper laugh and Flora smiled ruefully. He put his hand on the terrace wall. Fairy lights strung between trees in the garden made the space look like a magical wonderland.

He said, 'I don't think I'll have to worry about you handling yourself with the vultures.'

Flora shrugged. 'They never scared me. They're just snobs.'

Vito turned to face her, with his back to the wall. 'What does scare you?'

Flora knew exactly what scared her. But she was reluctant to divulge it to Vito. But then she thought, he now knew her more intimately than anyone else… She looked at him. 'I'm scared of being invisible.'

He didn't say anything for a long moment and then he glanced over her head behind them and said, 'I don't think that's something you'll have to worry about any more.'

She looked behind her to see most of the crowd gawking at them. She blushed. She wanted to bury her head in Vito's chest and that surprised her. Since when had he become a safe harbour?

'They're just bored and looking for a scandal.'

Vito reached for her and pulled her close. She fell into him with a muted swish of layers of fabric. He was tall and solid. *Hard.* Flora's blush got hotter.

He said, 'Then let's give them what they want, hm?'

And then he kissed her, blocking everything out, including the fact that she'd just revealed to him her worst fear, cultivated after growing up in a house with people who hadn't seen her. Who'd all but stepped over her.

It had been a long time since she'd felt noticed or seen and the fact that it was happening here with the sworn enemy of her family was too much to get her head around right now. So she pushed it aside and revelled in Vito's desire, because she was aware of another fear developing—the moment when he would look at her and not see her or want her any more.

Hours later, in Vito's bed, Vito was somewhere between waking and sleeping. Flora was a soft and delicious weight against him, one leg thrown over his thighs. He waited for a feeling of claustrophobia. It didn't come. Only the hunger.

They certainly had caused a stir earlier that evening. Flora had captivated the crowd in a way that had taken even him by surprise. Not because he'd underestimated her beauty but because he could see how her innate goodness shone out and took people unawares.

She'd defused the cynicism in the room without even opening her mouth. It had evoked something in him that he hadn't ever felt with a woman before. A need to protect. Against the women who would chew her up and spit her out so fast her head would be spinning and the men who wanted her.

So, actually, Vito had felt two things. Protective and possessive.

His mind cast around desperately for reasons why she evoked these things in him.

*It was the guilt.*

He felt a sense of relief. That was it. The guilt he carried for having sent her out to the streets. Even though she didn't hold him accountable. He'd almost prefer it if she did.

Earlier, on their way back to his apartment, in the car, she'd asked him, 'So what is it that scares you? Not much, I'd imagine.'

Vito had instinctively felt the need to close up, shut

down the conversation, but then he'd recalled her fear of being invisible and how that had struck him deep. He'd felt something similar when his parents had died and he'd suddenly been on his own in the world, without a family. With nothing but his name and the clothes on his back. And revenge in his heart. Having to somehow resurrect himself from the pit of grief and loss.

He'd felt her looking at him with those big gold-flecked eyes. So he'd admitted it, that his fear was of losing everything. Again.

She'd said, 'That's why you don't want a family?'

Vito had countered, 'That's why I choose to focus on my business because no matter what happens, even if I lost it all tomorrow… I won't be destroyed. Things and businesses can be rebuilt, people can't.'

He'd looked at her then, her face in shadow. He'd asked, 'Do you remember your family at all?'

She'd shaken her head. 'No, not that much. I was very young.'

Vito wasn't sure he entirely believed her but he wasn't about to delve into any more personal territory. He was only interested in the physical. Not the emotional or psychological. When they had arrived back at the apartment Vito had taken Benji from Flora and said, 'I'll take him out, you get ready for bed. *My* bed.'

When he'd arrived back and gone into his bedroom he'd seen the evening gown carefully draped over a chair and the jewellery neatly lined up on the dresser. Something about that had caught at him, which had annoyed him.

He hadn't been able to see Flora. But then the curtain by the French doors had moved and he'd gone over to see her standing with her arms on the wall, in a robe, bare feet. Not waiting for him seductively in the bed, like another lover. But here, enjoying the view. That little clutch at his chest again…

Flora moved now beside him in the bed, bringing him back from the ledge of his thoughts. She slid a hand across his chest, nails snagging on a nipple. Vito sucked in a breath. Even now, he felt the impulse to put some distance between them, to send her back to her own bed, to set boundaries…but now her mouth was on his skin and he felt the wet heat of her tongue and the impulse died a fiery death.

She knew where he stood, he'd told her in no uncertain terms there was no possibility of a long-term relationship with him, so why not let the boundaries blur and enjoy the moment?

He drew her up and over him, so her entire body lay over his, breasts against his chest. He could feel the scrape of her nipples. Her hair fell around them in a wild curtain of waves and curls. She looked sleepy but delicious.

He said, 'Open your legs.'

She did, her thighs going either side of his hips. With his hands and mouth and then his whole body, he brought them to the edge and back countless times, until their skin was slick and Flora was begging incoherently for release, and only then did he thrust so deep that they both fell together in a cataclysm of pleasure so intense that any sense of control Vito had wielded for those brief moments while staving off this pleasure felt like a very hollow victory.

# CHAPTER EIGHT

'WOULD YOU LIKE to go to New York?'

Flora looked at Vito from the other side of the dining table where they were having breakfast. A spoon upon which was heaped granola, fruit and yoghurt was stopped halfway to her mouth.

'Seriously?'

He nodded and wiped his mouth with a napkin. 'I'm opening a new office there and I've been invited to some social events.'

Flora put the spoon back down. There was a fizzing excitement in her belly. 'I've always wanted to go to New York.'

'Well, then, you'll just need your passport. We'll be leaving tomorrow.'

The fizzing excitement leached away. Flora sagged back. 'I don't have a passport.'

Vito looked incredulous but then his expression darkened. 'Let me guess, your beloved uncle didn't deem it necessary because he didn't allow you to go anywhere.'

'Something like that. It's been on my list of things to do but I hadn't got around to it yet.' Flora felt pathetic. Who didn't have a passport? 'I won't be able to go.'

Vito shook his head. 'Yes, you will. You'll come with

me right now to my office and we'll do whatever it takes to arrange a passport.'

'But that can't be done in a day.'

Vito arched a brow. 'There's not much I can't achieve in a day.'

Now Flora felt stupid. As if a bit of bureaucratic red tape would stand in Vittorio Vitale's way.

'Are you sure? I don't want to cause work for you and your employees.'

Vito held out a hand. 'Come here.'

Flora's heart palpitated at the look in his eyes. She still couldn't really believe that she was here, with this man, and that last night she'd been dressed like a princess from a fairy tale—a fairy tale that had turned into something much more X-rated when they'd arrived back at the apartment.

She got up from her chair and let Vito take her hand, pulling her onto his lap. He said, 'I know I asked you if you wanted to come to New York but it wasn't really a question. I need you there.'

Flora's heart fluttered, but before she could lose herself in a little daydream Vito was saying, 'After all, we have a plan to execute—show everyone that we're a couple.'

She went a little cold inside, even though Vito's arms were around her waist. 'Of course,' she said as lightly as she could. She extricated herself from his embrace and went back to the other side of the table again. 'How could I forget?'

She didn't look at him but she could feel his gaze on her as she studiously ate some of her breakfast.

'Flora…'

Reluctantly she looked up. He said, 'You need to understand that this is just a temporary thing…for as long as we want each other. That hasn't changed. The sex between us is…intense, but it's just sex. I won't want more and when the time comes we will be moving on with our lives. I will make sure you're set up. That's the least I can do for you after—'

Flora put up her hand. Vito stopped talking. She hid the dangerous pang near her heart because she *did* need to hear him spell this out. Because she knew deep down that his effect on her had already impacted her emotionally in a way that she feared was more comprehensive than she liked to admit.

She said, 'I've just gained my independence and freedom. I won't be giving that up for anyone for a long time. If ever. The man who will persuade me to one day consider entering into a relationship will have to be very special, someone I can trust. You don't have to worry, Vito. I know exactly the type of man you are, and I might have been sheltered all my life but I'm not so naive or self-destructive to think for a second that you'll ever want more than this affair.'

Vito didn't say anything for a long moment and then, 'You don't trust me.'

Flora's eyes widened, he sounded almost…*hurt*. Ridiculous. The man was impervious to anything she could ever inflict on him. 'I do trust you. I trusted you with my innocence, didn't I? But don't worry, I would have to be the biggest idiot on the planet to trust you with my heart.'

Vito stared broodingly across the plane to where Flora was curled up on a seat, asleep. Benji was a fluffy ball beside her. She'd looked so crestfallen when he'd said the dog couldn't come to New York that he'd suddenly found himself moving mountains to make it work, ensuring Benji had all the right documentation, vaccinations and health checks.

Flora was wearing new clothes supplied by the stylist, soft black leather skinny trousers and a cream silk shirt. Her hair was loose. Feet bare.

But all Vito could think about was what she'd said the day before: *'I would have to be the biggest idiot on the planet to trust you with my heart.'*

Her words should have made him feel assured that the little telltale dreamy look he'd seen in her eyes didn't mean that she was confusing amazing sex with emotion.

But instead of feeling assured, or relieved, he'd felt… unsatisfied. Unsettled.

She'd spoken of meeting a man some day who she could trust enough to be in a relationship with. Ridiculously, Vito had felt insulted that she evidently didn't consider him trustworthy. And worse, he'd felt an almost violent sense of rejection at the image of her with another man.

He wasn't used to feeling possessive of a lover. To the point of almost…jealousy.

He shook his head at himself now. No, it wasn't jealousy, because as soon as this desire burnt out he would be ready to let her go, to find this man she could trust with her heart.

This relationship with Flora was different from anything he'd ever experienced before because of what had happened six months ago. They had a history. And Vito had been instrumental in Flora being put in a perilous situation for the last six months.

He was ensuring that she would not be in that position again—he owed her that much. The fact that they shared this crazy chemistry was something neither of them could have foreseen. It would burn out soon, it always did, and then they would both have got what they wanted from this brief interlude and they could get on with their lives.

The dog lifted its head at that moment and looked balefully at Vito, as if he'd heard his thoughts and was warning him to tread very carefully.

Vito rolled his eyes at himself. He was losing it. He opened up his laptop again and resolved to focus his attention on work but then Flora's husky-sounding voice said, 'Where are we? Was I asleep for long?'

Vito looked over. She was deliciously tousled and sleepy. She stretched, which made the silk shirt ride up, exposing her belly.

Desire surged and Vito mentally cursed her for messing with his head. He closed his laptop and said, 'We're about halfway, which is perfect timing.'

She looked at him. 'Timing for what?'

He stood up and held out a hand. 'To show you where the bedroom is.'

She frowned. 'But I just had a nap—' She stopped and blushed. 'Oh.'

'Oh,' Vito echoed, his blood pumping at the thought of introducing Flora to the decadent side of private air travel.

Flora put Benji down into his dog bed on the floor and slipped her hand into his. Vito pulled her up and led her down to the back of the plane, telling himself that the more he indulged this desire, the sooner it would burn out.

'Wow, just…wow.' Flora's eyes didn't feel big enough to take in the entire view spread out before her. Central Park, surrounded by the iconic sky-scraping tall, elegant buildings. One of which she was at the top of, on a terrace. The streets were far below, the sounds of the traffic barely piercing through to the atmosphere up here.

She tore her eyes off the view for a moment to look up at Vito, who was staring at her. She flushed. 'I must seem like such a hick to you.'

He shook his head and turned to look out at the view too. 'No, everyone should have this reaction when seeing one of the world's most famous views for the first time.'

'Did you?'

Vito's mouth quirked. 'I hate to say it but probably not. I was so consumed with restoring my father's good name and making sure I was on your uncle's tail that I'm sure I barely glanced at this view.'

Flora felt a pang near her heart at the thought of Vito being so driven in his quest to mete out justice that he hadn't even looked around him to see the beauty of the world he was conquering.

Her body still felt heavy and also sensitised after what had happened on the flight. They'd been asleep in the bed after making love and the attendant had had to wake them as they were due to land shortly. Flora had been so mortified at their decadence that she hadn't been able to look any of the staff in the eye.

Vito had looked at her with a smile around his mouth,

and the thought of him being amused because he'd done this a hundred times before with other women had had Flora picking up a magazine to throw at him. He'd merely laughed then.

Benji was zipping around on the terrace full of beans after the flight. Flora welcomed the diversion from thinking too much about how Vito made her feel. 'Can I take him to the park for a walk?' She had a sudden vision of Vito accompanying them. Like some sort of real happy couple.

Vito said, 'Of course. You can do whatever you want, Flora. The city is yours.' He put out a hand.

Flora gulped. The thought of being able to move around in a city like this as if she had some sort of right to be there and take up space was daunting.

'I think I'll just take him to the park…' Feeling shy—which was ridiculous when she could still feel his hands on her body—Flora said, 'Are you busy now? You could come with us…'

Vito shook his head, suddenly turning brisk. 'I have to go straight to the offices to meet with the managers.'

It was early afternoon in New York and Flora's stomach rumbled. She hadn't eaten much on the plane. Vito said, 'The chef here will prepare you some lunch.'

Embarrassed at her very normal bodily functions, Flora said, 'It's fine, I'll find a hot-dog stand or get a pizza slice.'

'You have your mobile phone?'

Flora patted her back jeans pocket. 'Yes, sir, all programmed in with all your numbers and your assistant's number.'

'Call me if you get lost or if anything happens. Straight away.'

Flora looked at Vito and rolled her eyes. 'I might not have been here before but I'm not completely clueless in a city. Rome is pretty big and cosmopolitan, you know.'

To her surprise he took her chin in his forefinger and thumb and planted a swift kiss on her mouth. It burned. He drew back, eyes dark, unfathomable. 'I'll see you later. We have a cocktail party to attend on the other side of the park. My house manager will unpack the bags and I've arranged for a glam team to come at five to help get you ready.'

Flora felt simultaneously hurt at the thought that she evidently needed so much help but also desperately relieved that she didn't have to try and tame her wayward hair or do her own make-up.

'Okay, see you later.'

And then he was gone, taking his force field of energy and charisma with him. Flora breathed out. The thought of a walk in the park and some respite from Vito wasn't altogether a bad thing.

'Stop fidgeting.'

Flora sighed at Vito's admonishment and dropped her hand from the hem of the dress.

She whispered at Vito in the back of the car, mindful of the driver in the front. 'It's too short.'

Vito put his hand over Flora's on her thigh and said, 'It's the perfect length. And you weren't worried about the length of your dress when you went to that club looking for your first lover.'

Flora's face burned. No, she'd been completely wanton. 'This is different,' she pointed out. 'We're not going to a nightclub.'

'And you're not looking for a lover any more.'

Heat filled Flora's body. No, she wasn't looking for a lover. She had *a lover*. The thought was still thrilling.

Vito curled his hand around Flora's bare thigh. He said, 'Want me to show you how perfect your dress is?' His hand moved up her thigh, pushing the hem of the dusky pink cocktail dress up even higher.

Flora put her hand on his. She whispered, 'We can't, the driver.' But an illicit electric charge was already making her ready for Vito's touch.

He issued a command that Flora barely heard and within seconds a privacy window had gone up between them and the driver. He turned to face her and pulled her closer. Flora was only aware of him and this space cocooning them from the outside world.

Vito's mouth covered hers and she allowed him full access, her whole body vibrating with desire as his tongue touched hers. His hand crept higher up her thigh and tacitly Flora opened her legs wider.

She could hear Vito's hum of approval in the back of his throat and she felt a jolt of pure adrenalin when his fingers pushed aside the flimsy gusset of her underwear and stroked into her with expert precision.

Flora gasped into Vito's mouth as his fingers worked to bring her to a rapid and shuddering climax, her whole body trembling in the aftermath.

As much as it excited her that he could do this to her, it also scared her a little. It was as if once he touched her she wasn't remotely in control of her own autonomy. She opened her eyes and was mildly comforted to see the stark look of hunger on Vito's face. On an impulse she put her hand on him, where his body was hard under his trousers. She suddenly felt audacious. His eyes glittered. He said, 'If we weren't just minutes away from our destination I wouldn't stop you.'

Flora took her hand away and straightened herself as much as she could. She stored up the fact that there were things she could do to push this man off his axis as much as he did to her. Maybe on the way home…

'What are you thinking?'

Flora looked at Vito, affecting an innocence that this man had stripped her of with her full consent. 'Nothing at all.'

Flora heard him mutter something that sounded like *temptress* and resolved there and then to definitely turn the tables on him on the way home. But first she had to navigate an upmarket social event and she just prayed that the stylist who'd told her to wear this strapless thigh-skimming cocktail dress wasn't sending her out to make a fool of herself.

The cocktail party was taking place on the rooftop of one of the tall buildings almost directly opposite Vito's apartment on the other side of the park. The crowd here was different from in Rome, a little more relaxed. Flora was relieved to see that she was far from the only woman baring so much skin.

People here were curious about her but they didn't have the same intense interest as the people in Rome, understandably.

The entire terrace had been set up for the party and was being hosted by one of New York's grand dames.

'It's basically a very exclusive networking opportunity,' Vito had told Flora when she'd asked the purpose of the party.

There were delicious-looking canapés, but each time a waiter appeared Flora resisted the urge to taste one, knowing that she'd end up with caviar down her chest or some other catastrophe.

Vito was locked in conversation with a couple of other men and Flora was staring wistfully at another tray of canapés leaving her sight.

'I get it, too nervous to eat in case it goes everywhere?'

Flora turned to the woman behind the voice. A beautiful blonde woman with her hair swept up in an elegant chignon, exactly the kind of up-do Flora could never achieve.

She smiled ruefully. 'It's that obvious?'

The woman—who sounded English—chuckled and gestured to her own classic sheath of a sleeveless dress in a light cream colour. 'Let's just say I can empathise. Tell you what, I'm starving because I didn't have lunch, we only arrived in from London today, so why don't we go and eat together and then we can make sure we're still presentable?'

Flora grinned. She hadn't expected to meet someone so friendly in a place like this. 'Deal,' she said and let the woman lead her away from Vito to where caterers had a table set up groaning under a veritable feast of food.

'Who was the woman you were talking to during the party?'

Flora turned to Vito in the back of the car. 'I'm sorry, was I meant to stay by your side? I was just hungry and so was she and I was too scared to eat any of the canapés in case I spilled something and so was she and so—'

Vito put a finger to Flora's lips. He shook his head. 'I don't expect you to stay by my side. You're a free agent.'

He could feel Flora's breath against his finger and he got hard. He pulled his hand back, cursing her effect on him. Cursing her for distracting him all evening—either when she'd been beside him, with her scent and presence and her body, poured into a dress that emphasised her tiny waist and shapely hips and generous breasts, or even worse when she hadn't been beside him. When she'd been talking to someone else.

'That's good,' she said. 'If I ever went to a social event with my uncle, say if my aunt was ill, or away, he'd expect me to stay right beside him and remember everyone we talked to. He'd quiz me on the way home.'

Vito's conscience pricked. 'Like I am now?'

Flora shook her head, making tendrils of her hair move around her face. Her hair hadn't been straightened, but it had been pulled back into a low bun. Acting on instinct, Vito said now, 'Turn around.'

She did, giving him her back. Of course he was immediately tempted to pull the zip of her dress down, but he resisted. He wasn't a teenager. *Maledizione.*

He pulled the pins out of her hair and it slowly loosened and fell down her back and around her shoulders.

'Oh, that feels so good,' she murmured.

Vito speared his fingers in her hair and massaged her skull. She groaned softly and that only made him harder. He gritted his jaw.

'So, the woman? I'm just curious because she looked familiar.'

'Her name is Carrie Black—'

Vito's hands stopped moving. Flora turned her head. 'Do you know her?'

'She's the wife of the man I'm hoping to do some business with, Lord Massimo Black. He's primarily a philanthropist but he does invest in choice businesses. What were you talking about?'

He could see Flora bite her lip. She turned to face him more fully now. 'Just chit-chat really. She was lovely.'

Flora suddenly looked nervous. 'Actually…she recognised me.'

'How?'

'They'd been in Rome when the wedding…didn't happen. The paparazzi didn't get any shots of me afterwards but the tabloids had some old pictures of me from something with my uncle. When she realised I was here with you she said she hoped I'd made you grovel for what you'd done.'

Vito couldn't exactly fault her sentiment. The guilt he felt at all but throwing Flora out onto the streets was still like a burr under his skin. 'What did you say?'

'Something about you having your reasons.' Flora's mouth quirked. 'She said she hoped you were going to bring me to Tiffany's or Cartier for a suitably expensive grovel gift.'

Flora's mouth stopped quirking and she said quickly, 'I told her of course I wasn't into anything like that. And how you'd let me bring my dog to New York. She gave me her number and told me to call her if I wanted to meet up. She has her children here but she said a walk in the park might be nice some day.'

Vito thought of how he'd had a conversation with Massimo Black and the man had expressed interest in meeting Vito again to discuss things further. Meanwhile Flora had been exchanging numbers with his wife.

Normally when Vito brought a date to a social function, it was purely as an enhancement with the prospect of sating his libido. He'd certainly never experienced *this* kind of scenario: a woman actually helping him to foster other connections. It was disconcerting, because it made him realise that perhaps insisting on being a lone wolf was a weakness. And that having someone by his side in a more meaningful way could actually be an advantage, beyond just presenting a superficially more respectable image.

Flora said, 'I hope I didn't do or say anything to damage your relationship with Carrie's husband.'

Vito realised that she looked anxious. He shook his head. 'Not at all. And it's not your responsibility to be concerned for my image or business concerns.'

Now she looked embarrassed. 'Oh, of course, I know I have no influence.'

'Oh, you have influence, Flora, don't worry about that.' Vito reached for her and pulled her closer, leaving her in no doubt as to exactly how her influence affected him. 'You couldn't but be an asset to the people around you. You're a nice person, Flora Gavia, and that's a miracle considering who you had to grow up with.'

To Vito's surprise, Flora's eyes looked suspiciously bright. 'That's a really sweet thing to say.'

Vito felt a little winded for a moment. No one had ever accused him of being *sweet* before, certainly not a woman. He was acutely aware of Flora's relative naivety and innocence, not just physical, and once again he felt a sense of protectiveness that he couldn't stem, even though it unnerved him.

He assured himself again that, for all of that naivety though, she knew what was happening here and she had no false illusions. In fact, out of all the women he'd been with, she was the least likely to believe in fairy tales. They both had their respective past traumas to thank for that.

She looked shy now and her cheeks were pink. 'Actually, there was something I wanted to do earlier but we didn't have time…'

Vito recalled her hand on him, shaping his body, and he issued a command to put up the privacy window, but also to drive around until he told the driver differently.

He said, 'We have all the time in the world now.'

He watched as Flora, with her tongue between her teeth, set about freeing him from his trousers. He had to call on every ounce of control he possessed not to spill right there, watching as she took him in her hand and moved it up and down as if fascinated by the way he looked in her hand.

He was about to tell her to stop, he wouldn't be able to hold on and he would make a fool of himself, but now she was lowering her head and her breath was feathering over his sensitised flesh, and he had to put his head back and grit his teeth so hard it hurt as she wrapped her mouth around him and his universe was reduced to that hot sucking heat.

When Vito had fallen over the edge of pleasure and control and Flora came back up again, a very feminine smile on her face, Vito cursed himself for ever thinking she was naive or innocent. She was no such thing.

She was a temptress through and through and he was an idiot to think otherwise.

When Flora woke the following morning she found she was getting used to the sensation of her body feeling heavy with a sensual lassitude. The night came back in fragments, the car on the way to the party, the way Vito had made her come apart, and then afterwards how she'd made *him* come apart. It had been intensely satisfying to see his face flushed, eyes glittering, looking at her as if she'd just stunned him.

But then, when they'd returned to the apartment, he'd shown her in no uncertain terms who was the master here. Undoubtedly him, in spite of her little victories.

She heard a sound and cracked open one eye to wince at the bright daylight flooding into the bedroom.

She opened both eyes and felt a small furry weight launch onto the bed, landing beside her. She snuggled Benji close.

'He's been fed and walked already, by Matthew, the housekeeper. You can go back to sleep.'

Flora looked up to see Vito standing in the doorway in a three-piece suit, hair still damp from a shower, jaw clean-shaven. He looked so gorgeous it almost hurt.

Feeling a little exposed and defensive, she said, 'I'm not usually so tardy. I'm blaming you for keeping me up late.' And yet he managed to get up, no problem. She came up on one elbow, holding the sheet to her chest.

Vito leaned against the doorframe with folded arms. 'There's a credit card in your name on the table in the hall. Go shopping or make an appointment with a spa and treat yourself. My assistant can book you in. You deserve a break, Flora. It's nothing to feel guilty about.'

For someone who'd lived her life feeling indebted to the people around her and being as useful as she could be to mitigate that feeling, it was totally counter-intuitive to her to put herself first.

Flora said dryly, 'I don't think there's much left to wax or buff.' She looked at him, wondering if she was missing some vital piece of 'mistress' behaviour. 'Unless you would like me to do...something else?'

She thought of the fact that she wasn't shaved *down there*, and blushed. He hadn't seemed to mind, but maybe—

But Vito was shaking his head and coming back over to the bed, sitting on the edge and reaching for the sheet, twitching it away to look at her. Her blood instantly got hot. He said, 'You are perfect. You don't need to do a thing. And, as tempting as you are, I'll have to resist for now. I have a meeting in half an hour.'

He got up again and Flora pulled the sheet back up, lamenting his control. Pushing him out of that control was fast becoming her favourite thing.

'See you later?' She hoped she didn't sound as eager as she felt.

He grimaced slightly. 'I have a business dinner later. You don't have to wait up.'

So Flora had a whole day stretching ahead of her to see this fascinating city and get her head around what this was with Vito. Not a bad prospect.

'Later, then.'

'Later.'

He looked at her so intensely for a moment that Flora

almost imagined that he couldn't help himself and would—but no, he was gone. She slumped back onto the bed. Benji crawled up and licked her face. She wrinkled her nose. 'Just us now, Ben, a whole day to explore and amuse ourselves.'

For the first time, because she was used to her own company, Flora felt a little hollow pang of loneliness. But before it could even register she pushed herself up and out of the bed, resolved to make the most of this amazing opportunity in one of the most iconic cities in the world.

After all, this affair with Vito was finite and she would have to get used to being on her own again, sooner rather than later, she had no doubt.

# CHAPTER NINE

WHEN VITO RETURNED that evening he felt wrung out, but also couldn't deny the frisson of anticipation that had been growing ever since he'd made his excuses from the most boring dinner on the planet to come back to the apartment. And now that frisson was getting stronger.

He entered the apartment, pulling open his tie and the top button of his shirt. Clothes had never made him feel as restricted as they had since he'd been with Flora Gavia. A unique experience, as if he just wanted to be naked all the time. He smiled a little grimly at that notion.

He made his way through the softly lit apartment looking for her. He noticed things. Some dog toys on the ground. A pair of her trainers. A top on the back of a chair. More flowers than he would usually have in the apartment. He stopped and looked around. It looked… lived in. A novel concept for Vito when he was used to moving through spaces he inhabited without leaving much of a ripple.

Disconcertingly, it appealed to him. It made him feel somehow— He heard a sound and he looked to the doorway leading to the bedrooms and every coherent thought went out of his head.

Flora was standing there, lit with a golden glow, in a simple but devastatingly provocative silk negligée with thin straps. With one flick of his finger it would fall away from her body.

He was hard in an instant.

She looked a little dishevelled. She'd been sleeping. She said, 'I thought I heard something.'

Vito regretted not bringing her to dinner. She would have made it so much more interesting. But she would have distracted everyone. *Him.* He walked towards her. 'What if I'd been an intruder?'

'I'm sure Benji would have barked the block down and alerted me.'

The dog in question looked up sleepily from his bed and put his head back down. The most ineffectual guard dog ever.

Vito was just a foot away from Flora now. Her hair was spilling over her shoulders, wild and making his fingers itch. But then he remembered something and put his hand in his inside jacket pocket. He pulled out a long slim box and handed it to Flora. 'For you. Carrie Black was right. You do deserve a grovelling gift.'

Flora looked shocked. And reluctant. 'You don't have to give me anything.'

'Will you take it if I tell you I went in and chose it myself?'

Now she looked curious. She saw the name on the box and sucked in a breath at the iconic jewellers. 'Vito, this is too much.'

'You haven't even looked at it yet.'

She eventually took it and opened it and sucked in another breath. Vito had actually gone into the shop on a whim earlier, when they'd been stuck in traffic and he'd spotted it.

He'd noticed this necklace almost immediately and he'd known she would love it. It was a simple gold flower, with delicate petals and a lustrous pearl in the centre, on a gold chain.

For a second he regretted choosing something so… personal. Why hadn't he just chosen a diamond bracelet or something more bland? Too late now.

Flora stroked it with a finger. 'Vito, it's lovely.' She looked up at him. 'How did you know?'

Now he felt a little exposed. He shrugged. 'I saw it and thought of you, your name. Flora, flower.'

He took the box from her and took out the necklace, holding it up. 'May I?'

Flora nodded and turned around, lifting her hair up and off her neck. Vito reached around in front of her and placed the necklace around her neck, closing the clasp.

When it was closed he brought her hands down and her hair fell back down. She turned around. The necklace sat just below the hollow of her throat on her pale golden skin. She touched it. 'Thank you, you really didn't have to do that, but I love it.'

Without even asking her, Vito already knew that her uncle and aunt had most likely been very negligent in giving her anything or marking occasions like birthdays. They'd been too busy fleecing her of her inheritance.

Vito put the empty box down and took Flora's hand, leading her back towards the bedroom. He'd given up trying to put a boundary between them by using two bedrooms. Easier just to give into the inevitable.

In the bedroom, he stripped off with efficient speed

and then he looked at Flora. The gold glinted against her skin. Vito found that, in spite of the sense of exposure, he liked seeing it there.

His gaze travelled down. The top of the slip rested just over her breasts. He could see the hard nubs of her nipples pressing against the fabric. He controlled himself though. It was important. To make him feel as though he weren't fraying at the edges and losing sight of what was important to him. Making an indelible success of the Vitale name so no one would ever question his father's integrity again. He couldn't think of that now. He'd worry about that later.

He looked down and could see the darker shadow of where the honey-golden curls covered her sex. He imagined her already hot there. Damp. *Ready.*

'Vito…' she said a little breathlessly. 'You're killing me here.'

He looked at her and moved closer. 'Good, because you're killing me too.'

He cupped one breast covered in that slippy silk and bent his head to target and suck the hard flesh of her nipple into his mouth. She gasped and speared her hands in his hair.

He caught her against him and she wrapped a hand around his straining flesh. Vito almost lost it there and then but somehow he managed to get them onto the bed, roll protection onto his length and finally sink into her slick tight embrace. It was fast and he couldn't control it. Vito felt Flora's body contract around his and he gave in, letting the pleasure take him where it wanted—to oblivion. Their bodies were so entwined that he couldn't have said where he ended and she began and, right then, he didn't care.

The following afternoon Vito was aware of the meeting continuing behind him. But he was brooding as he looked out of a window that commanded breathtaking views of downtown Manhattan. This *should* be a moment for him to really appreciate just how far he'd come and how successful he'd been in restoring the Vitale name.

But instead of feeling a sense of triumph he was distracted. Thinking of Flora's expression earlier at breakfast when he'd shot down her request to do something for him, to make herself useful.

She'd said, 'I had a nice time yesterday, it's not that I don't mind my own company, I'm used to it. But I just feel a bit…redundant. Maybe I could help? I'm good at office stuff, photocopying… I wouldn't mind getting teas and coffees. I'm not too proud.'

Vito had leaned over to her and pressed a swift kiss on her mouth before saying, 'You might not be, but I am. I'm not having my lover fetching tea and coffee for my staff.'

He'd stood up to leave. 'I'll be back in time for dinner this evening.'

Flora had perked up. 'I could cook.'

He'd reminded her that they had a chef to cook. She'd tried to hide it but Vito had been aware of her disappointment.

Didn't she get it? That it was enough for him that she be with him when he needed and in his bed when he wanted? That was all he asked of any woman he chose.

*But she's not like the other women.*

Ha! As if he needed that reminder. He'd bought her that necklace. He still felt exposed just thinking about it.

She'd said to him that morning before he'd left, 'I'm sure someone will have a use for me.'

Vito had been sorely tempted to remind her of exactly how useful she was, in his bed, but he'd resisted the urge. Partly because it had unnerved him, how strong it was to just…give into their mind-blowing desire.

He looked out over the city skyline. She was somewhere out there, in this vast city, on her own, doing… *something*. Making herself useful! And he was curious. Because he was sure that whatever she was doing would surprise him. Curious, and also a little envious if he was completely honest. For the first time since he could remember, work and his relentless ambition felt a little… hollow. The lure of being with Flora as she discovered the city was appealing. More than appealing.

He was so tempted to text her and check what she *was* doing that he deliberately didn't. Had he forgotten that she was a Gavia? And even though he was fairly certain now that she hadn't been involved in any of her uncle's nefarious activities, by allowing her to distract him like this, it was almost as if he were still allowing them to sabotage his business.

He turned away from the view and back to the meeting and said, 'Where were we?' and put all thoughts of Flora out of his head.

Three days later.

Vito was ready to admit defeat. He'd spent the last few days throwing himself into his work schedule in a bid to pretend that Flora wasn't taking up as much of his mental energy as she was.

But he was losing it. Not even slaking his lust with her in bed at night made up for the fact that, during the days, he'd more or less left her to her own devices and had then painted himself into such a corner with work that when they'd returned to the apartment last night after an event, he'd had to take an important work call.

When he'd finally managed to terminate it, blood humming with anticipation, he'd come to the bedroom to find Flora on the bed, in that silky negligée, but fast asleep. She'd looked like Sleeping Beauty, and as innocent.

Something had made him hold back from waking her. A sense of exposure that was becoming all too familiar. And the desperation that had clawed at him to have her. It was growing stronger. Not weaker.

But now he found that his need to know where she was and what she was doing was superseding everything else. Even work.

He rang his housekeeper and was informed that Flora was out. 'Doing what?' Vito asked as civilly as he could.

'Um… I believe she's walking dogs.'

'You mean *the* dog. Benji.'

'No,' his housekeeper responded, 'I mean *dogs*. She got talking to one of the neighbours the other day who was telling her she couldn't get out because she had a sprained ankle, so Flora offered to take her two dogs on her walk. By the time she came back from that walk, a couple more neighbours were asking her if she could walk their dogs too.'

Vito absorbed this. He terminated the call, feeling more distracted than ever. He turned to his manager. 'You have everything in hand for the rest of the day?'

'Of course, I'll call if anything comes up.'

Vito left, not even sure where he was going or what he was doing. He instructed his driver to take him back to his apartment. It was late afternoon anyway, so not entirely inconceivable that he'd be stopping for the day, but for him, a man whose single-minded focus had been on work since he was a teenager, it was a novel sensation.

The car pulled up outside the apartment building and Vito saw her. She was waiting to cross the road. His blood and pulse leapt. She looked…like a wild-haired nymph. She was wearing rolled-up jeans, a worn T-shirt—none of the sleek clothes the stylist had packed for her. Trainers.

And she was holding leads attached to at least six dogs. She crossed the road in front of the car and disappeared into the building. Vito got out and went up to the apartment.

When she returned with just Benji, presumably after dropping off the other dogs to their respective owners, Vito was waiting in the reception room. She saw him and stopped. She smiled. 'Hi. I didn't expect to see you back so early.'

Vito ignored the prick of his conscience at her obvious happiness to see him. 'Clearly. Were you going to tell me about your little entrepreneurial side hustle?'

Flora frowned. 'You mean the dogs? You saw me?'

Vito nodded. Her face flushed. He forced himself to focus and not think of making the rest of her body flush with desire.

Now Flora looked wary. 'What's wrong? Am I not allowed to help people?'

*Of course she is.*

'You're not charging them to walk their dogs?'

Now she looked disgusted. 'Of course not. They're your neighbours. And they're very nice. Mrs Weinberg sprained her ankle—'

Vito held up a hand. She stopped talking. He said, 'I'm sure they're lovely people. But you're not a dog-walker.'

Flora pushed some hair over her shoulder, agitated. 'I can be whatever I want to be.'

'I thought you wanted to be a graphic designer.'

Flora folded her arms across her chest. 'You don't want your...*lover* to be seen doing menial work. Is that it?'

Vito forced himself to sound unconcerned when the need to know everything she did suddenly seemed more compelling than anything else. 'I'm not a snob. I'm just curious. Indulge me.'

She threw her hands up. 'Because I was bored and I'm not used to sitting around doing nothing and I don't want to go shopping or to a spa. I want to be of use.'

Vito's hands itched to show her exactly how she could be of use.

She said, 'I did try to tell you, yesterday evening, but all those people wanted to talk to you at the event, and then you were on the phone when we got back and then... I fell asleep...and you didn't wake me.' Now she avoided his eye.

Vito didn't like the reminder of how he'd been overcome with duelling desires, to wake her and to walk away. She was fast becoming an obsession, if she wasn't already.

'I didn't want to disturb you,' he said now. A little voice mocked him. *Liar.*

Suddenly Flora looked shy and she said, 'I got something for you. Wait here.'

Vito watched her leave the room. Benji came over and sniffed around his feet but before he could cock his leg and mark his territory on Vito, he lifted him up and went to put him outside. The dog licked his face and Vito felt a little glow in his chest. He put him down on the terrace and pretended that the dog wasn't getting to him.

Vito went back inside and Flora was there, holding out a small black box. For some reason Vito had an almost superstitious reluctance to take it. No woman had ever bought him anything. Not since his mother had died.

But he couldn't ignore it. He took it and opened it to see silver cufflinks in the shape of eagles' heads, beautifully engraved.

Flora was saying, 'I saw them in the window of an antiques shop. They made me think of you, like an eagle, soaring above everything and biding your time until you could swoop down and take your vengeance for your father, and mother.'

It was uncanny but Vito had always had a fascination with birds of prey since he was a small child. He'd watched endless nature documentaries, much to his parents' bemusement because they lived in a city. But Vito had known that birds of prey stalked cities as much as out in the wild. He'd seen birds of prey high in the sky over Manhattan. The line between civilisation and nature was very thin.

The fact that Flora had picked these out made him feel acutely exposed, a sensation that was becoming far too familiar. He snapped the box shut. 'Thank you, but you really shouldn't have gone to the trouble.'

'It was no trouble.' Flora looked a little dejected but Vito was too full of conflicting emotions. Then she said quickly, 'I paid for them out of my own money,' and the emotions in Vito's chest and gut intensified.

He shook his head. 'You don't need to pay me back for anything, Flora.'

He was realising the full extent of just how far over and beyond the boundaries this situation had gone. Flora was like no other woman he'd ever been with. She was breaking all the rules and making up new ones. And through it all his blood was hotter for her than ever. The thought of this ending made him feel desperate. She wasn't out of his system yet. Surely it wasn't too late to restore some of those boundaries…

He handed back the box, even as bile rose from his gullet at what he was doing. 'You should return them and get your money back. I don't need anything.'

Flora's face became expressionless. Vito felt a cold finger trace down his spine. He had an urge to say, *No, wait, stop, I'm overreacting,* but Flora was already taking the box and putting it in her pocket. 'They were meant as a gift, not payment, but I should have realised that you'd be used to something a little more…sophisticated.'

She was turning away and Vito reached out and caught her arm. She turned back but avoided his eye. He tipped up her chin with his finger. Her eyes were guarded. He said, 'I don't mean to be ungrateful. It was a really thoughtful thing to do. Thank you.'

That sense of desperation was back but now it was because he wanted her to stop looking like a stranger. Unreadable. He took his hand down and said, 'How would you like to go to a show this evening? I don't have any engagements lined up.'

Flora shrugged minutely. 'Sure, that sounds nice.'

'Any show in particular?'

She smiled but Vito could see it was forced. The bile was almost choking him now. Flora said, 'Surprise me.'

So Vito did what he would normally do in a situation with a woman he was sleeping with—he went for the show that was the most in demand and the hardest to get tickets for. And even though that put him on ground that felt a little firmer, he knew that Flora was the one woman he couldn't impress so easily.

Flora was finding it hard to get swept away by the exuberant show on the stage, just feet from where they were sitting in a VIP box. She was still incredibly hurt after Vito handed back the present she'd got for him. She'd seen him look at the cufflinks with an arrested expression. But then his face had shuttered and he'd handed them back, and she'd felt like the biggest fool.

He'd proven that you really couldn't buy anything for the man who had everything. And he'd handed them back because he had obviously wanted to send her a message—don't cross the line. He'd managed to put her back in her place *and* remind her that her finances were paltry.

She should have taken the hint from the fact that she'd barely seen him for the last few days, clearly demonstrating his focus was on work and not on her.

And she shouldn't be hurt because if he had the ability to hurt her, it meant that he'd got a lot closer than she'd realised.

*Who are you fooling?* jeered a voice.

She knew it was already too late. He'd sneaked in under her skin and she was falling for him. And it was so humiliating because he'd stood her up at the altar in front of all of society, and the only reason he was still indulging her was because for some crazy reason he fancied her, but underneath that was the very obvious guilt he felt that he'd punished her along with her uncle. And she was still a Gavia. Vito would never commit to anything permanent with someone from his sworn enemy's family.

The minute he stopped fancying her, she'd be an unwelcome guest. There couldn't be less holding them together. Lust and guilt. And yet, as hurt as she was by his very obvious wish for her not to push the boundaries, he was the first person who had come into her life and seen her for herself, uniquely. Fatally, she knew she couldn't walk away. Not yet. His desire for her was calling to the deepest part of her where she'd locked herself away to avoid being hurt for so many years.

She was blooming to life under his gaze and even as she knew it was futile, all she could do was pray that he wasn't the only person who would ever make her feel like this. Desired. *Seen.* Because of one thing she was certain—Vittorio Vitale did not share the same depth of feelings.

That night when they returned to the apartment after the show, there was a silent intensity to their lovemaking, as if today had been a marker on the ground signifying that the end was nigh.

Flora shuddered against Vito as the powerful waves of her orgasm ripped through her body with Vito not far behind, his powerful body jerking in the throes of his own climax.

He lay over her, in her, for a long moment. Flora's legs and arms were wrapped around him and she knew she should move but she couldn't seem to. She knew that she was selfishly storing up these little moments so that she could take them out at a later date when this was all a distant memory.

Eventually, though, Vito pulled free of Flora's embrace but, to her surprise, he lifted her up and out of the bed with him, bringing her into the bathroom. He put her down gently and turned on the shower, the space filling with steam as the hot water ran.

He pulled her in with him and she protested weakly, 'My hair!'

Vito said, 'It's fine.'

Flora turned her face up to the spray, giving into Vito's ministrations as he washed her and her hair. His big hands running over every inch of her body, breasts, belly, hips, between her legs, until she was hot and slippery all over again.

When he was done, she lathered up her hands and explored his body, revelling in the freedom she had to trace her hands and fingers over hard muscles and powerful buttocks. And the muscle between his legs, standing stiff and proud. She wrapped a hand around him as his mouth found hers, and he put a hand between her legs, fingers seeking and finding where she ached, and together, with their breathing getting faster and faster, they came to climax again under the hot spray.

Afterwards, Vito's head was resting on the wall, over Flora's. He said with a half-chuckle, 'I didn't actually intend for anything but washing ourselves.' He moved back and tipped up her chin. Water was running in rivulets down his face and neck, onto his chest. Even though she was sated beyond anything imaginable, Flora already wanted to put her tongue there and follow them down his body.

'But,' he said, 'you're impossible not to touch, to want. What are you doing to me, woman?'

'I could say the same of you.' Flora felt prickly and vulnerable and still a little hurt after what had happened earlier.

Vito looked at her for a long moment but then broke the contact, turning off the water and moving out of the shower, taking a towel and wrapping it around Flora's body then taking another towel and rubbing her hair, before wrapping it up turban style.

Then Vito roughly dried himself, and, naked, led her back to the bed. She stopped in her tracks. 'I should probably go to my own room. My hair is damp.'

Vito looked at her. Flora's heart thumped. Since she'd been with him she'd shared his bed, his room. But now, maybe it was time to start putting some distance between them.

Vito's hand tightened on hers. She had a sense that he was going to agree with her, but then he said, 'You're not going anywhere, unless you want to.'

Putting it up to her. Flora knew she should break the contact, put some space between them, but fatally she heard herself saying, 'No, it's okay. I'll stay.'

They got back into the bed. A taut silence stretched between them. Flora was simultaneously deliciously tired but also energised. She also felt, after what had happened, and the way Vito had so brutally rejected her gift, a certain recklessness.

She turned on her side and put her head on her hand, studying him. But as she did, something inside her melted. His eyes were closed and his lashes were long on his cheeks. Face softened but no less stunningly handsome in rest. A hint of stubble lined his jaw. His nose was aquiline, and she wanted to trace its noble shape.

She thought of a small, dark-haired version of Vito, with his impenetrable eyes and intense nature, and to her surprise a yearning rose up inside her and it terrified her, because she'd never gone so far as to imagine having a family of her own. And what that would be like. The thought of it now felt akin to standing on the edge of a large canyon and taking a step out into thin air. Free-falling into space. With nothing to hold onto.

Vito made a small move and Flora tensed, imagining him waking and finding her like this—daydreaming of a future that could never be. But then he snored gently, indicating that he was already asleep, and Flora made a decision. She got out of the bed again, and silently made her way to the bedroom she'd never slept in. It was time to face up to the inevitable.

# CHAPTER TEN

'You weren't in the bed this morning.'

Flora avoided Vito's eye at the breakfast table. 'No, I, ah, felt bad about my hair getting the sheets damp so I moved into the other bedroom.'

'Is this going to be a regular occurrence?'

Flora forced herself to look at him and her heart flipped over. He was clean-shaven. She said, 'I think it's probably a good idea.'

After a long moment Vito said, 'You're probably right.'

Then Flora said mischievously, 'Actually, it's because you snore.'

Vito raised a brow. 'That's funny because so do you but I'd never be so rude as to mention it.'

Flora's mouth dropped open. 'No, I do not.'

'How would you know?' Vito pointed out.

Flora closed her mouth. She picked up a small pastry and threw it at him. He caught it deftly. He grinned and the flip-flopping of her heart got worse. Then Vito took another gulp of coffee, wiped his mouth and stood up, saying, 'By the way, we're leaving for London this afternoon. I have to stop off en route back to Rome. Is that okay?'

Flora looked at Vito. She felt as if she were on a roller

coaster, living at the speed of Vito. She nodded her head to indicate she didn't mind, even as the thought of London filled her with a sense of disquiet. She hadn't been back there since the accident that had killed her parents and brother, after they'd left her at a friend's house for a sleepover. She pushed it down deep where all the other painful memories were stored.

'How long will we be there?'

'Just a couple of days. There's an event to attend, and I'd like to meet with Massimo Black.'

Flora was slightly cheered at the prospect of seeing Carrie Black again. Then she thought of something. 'Oh, I promised Mrs Weinberg I'd take the dogs out again this morning and do a little shopping for her.'

Vito looked amused. 'You do realise that anyone living in this building can afford to have their dogs walked and their shopping bought whenever they want?'

Flora just smiled sweetly. 'Maybe they do, but maybe they're also just lonely and want a bit of human contact. Is that so bad?'

Vito shook his head and came around to her chair and bent down, putting his hands on the arms, caging her in. Flora's pulse leapt.

Vito said, 'You're too good to be true…or are you?'

'What's that supposed to mean?'

Vito shook his head and stood up again. The implication that she was somehow faking being nice cut Flora deeper than it should. Damn him.

She said, 'Don't you get tired of being so cynical all the time? Maybe things…and people are just as they seem.'

Vito's expression hardened. 'Maybe, in some small corner of the world, but not in my world.'

Now Flora felt sad. 'Then your world must be a very lonely place.'

A glint came into Vito's eye. 'Not so lonely…for now.' And on that, he turned and left the room. Those two words rang in Flora's head for the rest of the morning: *For now...for now.* As if Vito hadn't already made it clear as a bell that this was very finite, the message had just been well and truly drummed home.

London sweltered in the humid heat and under moody grey skies. A storm was imminent. To Flora, the weather felt as if it were an outward manifestation of the storm brewing inside her. The storm that told her all of this—between her and Vito—would explode sooner or later and she'd be left in the debris, shattered and hoping that she could pick herself up and start again.

Feeling maudlin, and not liking it because she strove hard to maintain a sunny attitude, Flora looked around the suite at the top of one of London's most iconic and exclusive hotels. She *should* feel as if she was fitting in. After all, she'd chosen her travelling clothes with care—cream pencil trousers and a matching silk blouse—pulled her hair back into a tidy braid because Vito had warned her about the British paparazzi because apparently they kept an eye on private planes arriving at the airport, hoping to catch celebrities.

Flora had almost forgotten about all of that thanks to the relative anonymity in America.

The suite was luxurious. Sumptuous. Thick plush carpets. Muted grey- and gold-trimmed decor that allowed the art and antiques to shine. Exquisite furniture.

But somehow all of this opulence only made her feel

unkempt and volatile. As if this world were mocking her, saying, *You never really belonged, not even with your uncle...*

Just then, Benji came into the room, and started sniffing around the leg of a chair that looked as if it had been in Louis XVI's court and, before he could cock his leg, Flora scooped him up and brought him out to the terrace.

When she'd put the dog down, Flora realised what it was that was bugging her, apart from being back in London after all these years, and the fact that she was falling for a man who saw her only as a lover and a vehicle to restore his reputation.

While Vito did make her feel seen in a way that was dangerously seductive, she also felt a bit like a piece of flotsam and jetsam being carried along in his current and at any moment, much like the way he'd announced they were coming to London, he might simply announce—

At that moment, as if conjured out of her tumultuous emotions, Vito appeared in the doorway. He was wearing a shirt and trousers. Casual. He looked up at the sky. 'It's starting to rain. You should come in.'

But Flora stayed rooted to the ground, emotions bubbling up before she could stop them. 'I don't have to do anything.'

Vito looked at her. 'There's a downpour starting.'

'So? It's only rain.'

Vito's gaze narrowed on her. He stepped out onto the terrace. 'Flora…what's going on?'

She struggled to articulate what she was feeling and finally she blurted out, 'I'm not just some sort of doll that you can pick up and put down and move around.'

Rain was falling now and it was heavy. Vito was shaking his head, hair beginning to flatten against his skull. He said, 'That's the last thing I think of you.'

They were getting drenched already, in just seconds, but Vito didn't seem inclined to move. Flora had to raise her voice over the rain. 'You just…need to give me notice, okay?'

'Notice of what?'

She bit her lip. 'Notice of when you don't want me any more. When it's over. You can't just announce it one morning, that you're done with me. Over breakfast.'

'Maybe you'll be done with me before I'm done with you,' Vito said. Flora absorbed that notion, as unlikely as she knew it was.

She said, 'Maybe I will, maybe you'll wake up one morning and I'll be gone.' Moving on with her life, going after her dreams and goals, even if they were still a little hazy. Flora had a sense of appreciation in that moment of how she'd survived in those first days after the wedding debacle. She could do it again, and she would. Perversely, the man who she knew would inevitably cause her untold emotional pain was also the person helping to remind her of her own agency and strength. A contradiction she didn't want to untangle right now.

Vito moved closer then, putting his hands on her waist, hauling her into him. She could feel every hard sinew of his powerful form. Their clothes were plastered to their bodies by now. The sky flashed with lightning and thunder rolled.

Vito said, 'No way, you're mine.'

Flora reached her arms up and wound them around his neck, arching herself against him. 'For now,' she said, echoing his words back to him but, even as she was reminded of her own strength, she hated to admit that she didn't feel as if she'd won any kind of victory.

She pressed her mouth to his and his hands speared in her hair, holding her in place so he could plunder her and stamp his very essence onto her. He lifted her then and brought her out of the rain and through the suite to the bedroom, and their sodden clothes were peeled off. He stood before her, every muscle sleek and taut, and she lay back on the bed. 'Make love to me, Vito.'

He came over her on two hands, and she opened her legs to him. He said as he joined their bodies in one single cataclysmic thrust, 'You're mine, Flora. *Mine.*'

She was his, for now, and he was hers, and she revelled in his possession, knowing that it wouldn't last.

The following day, Vito was distracted in his meeting. He'd given up trying to fool himself that he could avoid thinking about Flora. He texted her to see where she was—she'd mentioned going for a walk with Benji that morning. They had a function to attend that evening and he'd arranged for a glam team to meet Flora at the hotel. Even though he usually preferred how she looked before they teased her hair into some sort of up-do and put make-up over her freckles.

The after-effects of making love to Flora after that rainstorm lingered in his blood and body. He hadn't been able to get her words out of his head or the intensity of the way she'd said them.

*'I'm not just some sort of doll...'* and *'Maybe you'll wake up one morning and I'll be gone.'*

When Vito had woken that morning, to find Flora curled against his back, one arm draped over his waist, a hand splayed on his belly, he'd put his hand over hers and he hated to admit it, but he'd felt a sense of relief and he'd thought to himself, *Not today.*

But he wasn't fooling himself. It might not be today but it would be one day. Either he would end it because he would look at her and not want her, or maybe she *would* be the one to leave. And shouldn't Vito welcome that? After all, it wasn't as if he wanted anything more with this woman.

'Vito?'

Vito looked around. He hadn't even realised that his thoughts had propelled him up out of his seat and to a window. His phone pinged and he looked at it. A message from Flora with a location pin to a residential street in Mayfair. He frowned. What was she doing at a house in Mayfair?

He turned to the people around the board table. 'Can we wrap this up? I have somewhere I need to be.'

The fact that Vito was speeding through a meeting that would normally have absorbed one hundred per cent of his attention barely impinged now. He needed to go to Flora.

Flora was standing in the back garden when she felt the little hairs rise up on her arms. *Vito.* He'd come. She hadn't expressly asked him to but on some level she'd wanted him to come.

He came and stood beside her and asked, 'Are you interested in buying this house?'

Flora shook her head. 'No, of course not. They were having an open viewing. I had no idea it was up for sale.'

'So...why are you here?'

Flora swallowed. 'It was my home, with my parents and brother. I grew up here for eight years. After they died…my uncle sold it and the proceeds went into my inheritance.' She made a face. 'Well, what *would* have been my inheritance.'

Vito came and stood in front of her, obstructing her view of the large verdant garden. Benji ambled around nearby, sniffing the border hedging.

Flora forced herself to look at Vito, but her chest was tight and she was afraid of the emotion swelling up inside her. It had affected her more than she'd thought, when she'd first seen the number on the house and realised that the one for sale was her family home. She'd gravitated there without even knowing what she was doing.

Vito said quite seriously, 'Do you want it, Flora? I can buy it for you.'

A half-strangled laugh came out and she put her hand to her mouth before lowering it. She shook her head. 'No, I don't want the house. To be honest, I don't even remember all that much. A lot of my life here… I think I blanked it out afterwards. It was too painful to remember. We were so happy here. Me, and my parents and my little brother. But sometimes I think it can't possibly have been that perfect.'

She saw something beyond Vito and she grabbed his hand. 'I need to check something.'

She brought him down the garden to a tree at the end. Old and gnarly. She let his hand go and crouched down and pushed some leaves aside. When she saw what she was looking for on the trunk she felt a moment of pure happiness. She said, 'Look, it's still here.'

Vito bent down beside her. 'What am I looking at?'

Flora traced her finger over the etched words and spoke them out loud. '*"Flora and Charlie and Truffles."* I carved this not long before the accident.'

'Who was Truffles?' he asked.

'Our dog, a big shaggy golden retriever. I had to leave him in London. My uncle wouldn't let me take him to Rome.'

Vito stood up from his crouched position. Flora sensed his bristling energy. When she stood up his face was thunderous. She said, 'What's wrong?'

His eyes were obsidian. Flora shivered a little. It reminded her of how he'd looked in his office when she'd confronted him after the wedding debacle. He said, 'What your uncle did to you—it makes me want to go after him all over again and pound him to dust, make sure that he will never—'

Flora put her hand on Vito's arm. 'He doesn't deserve your anger or any more of your energy.'

Vito shook his head. 'Why are you *not* angry?'

'Because I didn't have that luxury for a long time. I depended on him solely. And it wasn't his fault that my parents and brother died, that was a freak accident on a rainy night after they'd left me at a friend's house. If anything, it was more my fault than his.' Flora admitted the thing she'd tortured herself with for years—if she hadn't wanted to go to her friend's house that night then maybe…

Vito was shaking his head. 'Not your fault. And it certainly wasn't your fault that your uncle then stole your inheritance.'

Flora shrugged. 'Money hasn't ever been that important to me.'

'Maybe because you felt you didn't deserve it? For living when they didn't?'

Vito's words stabbed Flora right in the heart. How could this man, who so coldly and cruelly handed her a public humiliation of the worst kind—standing her up on their wedding day—also be able to intuit one of her deepest and most shameful fears?

'Maybe,' she had to concede sadly. 'Why should I have benefited from an inheritance that my brother would never see because he was dead?'

'Why shouldn't you? I didn't know them but I'm fairly certain they wouldn't have wanted you deprived of it.'

Flora wanted to get Vito's suddenly far too perceptive focus off her. She walked away from the tree, leaving it behind. She asked, 'If your parents hadn't died... would you be different, do you think? Would you have achieved so much?'

'Who knows? Circumstances shape us into what we are, what we want. Maybe if my father hadn't been ruined I wouldn't have had the same hunger to succeed.'

Flora wrinkled her nose. 'You're ambitious... I think you would have still ended up where you are.'

'Maybe you're right, but I think I would have come up against your uncle sooner or later. He couldn't handle any competition. He would have come after me.'

She sneaked a look at Vito. He still looked ridiculously sexy even against this very domestic backdrop. Curious, she asked, 'Are you happy now that you've got your revenge?'

He stopped walking, as if her question had surprised him. 'I can't say it feels all that different apart from the fact that I'm not so consumed with one thing. If anything…it's been a bit of an anticlimax.'

'That's probably delayed grief. I can't imagine you took much time after your parents' deaths to grieve?'

He started walking again. 'Did you?'

'I was eight. I didn't know which way the world was up. I know that I didn't cry. Not for a long time.'

'But you did cry?'

Flora's chest squeezed. She nodded. 'Eventually, in quiet moments.' Wanting to move away from the painful subject of grief, Flora asked, 'Would you have had a family by now if you hadn't lost everything? If you hadn't been so intent on seeking justice?'

Vito shook his head. 'It never really interested me. I never felt it as a lack, as something that would fill a gap. My father, even before things got bad, was a workaholic. We spent a lot of time together primarily because he would take me to work with him. My mother hid it, but she was sad. I think they couldn't have more children and she never really got over it. So we were very tight. A unit. They loved me and I loved them. I didn't miss siblings so I've never particularly wanted children. I don't think I'd be a very good father.'

He'd more or less told her this already. She felt as if she was pushing for something, not even sure what. For him to admit that maybe he wanted more out of life than being a lone wolf? And that he wanted her to be a part of that?

He turned to face her, blocking out the few other people who were still in the garden. He asked, 'What about you?'

It hit her then, like a ton of bricks, standing here in

the back garden of her family home, surrounded by bittersweet memories. She said, almost to herself, 'Yes… I want a family. Some day. I'd like to try and recreate that happiness, in spite of the grief and fear of loss.'

'I'm sure you'll get it too, Flora. You'd deserve it. But I'm a selfish man, I want what I want and it's not that.'

Flora tried to ignore the way her insides clenched as if in rejection of his assertion. Her future wasn't bound with this man. She tipped up her chin. 'And what do you want?'

He reached for her. 'Haven't I been making myself very clear? I want you, Flora.'

She went into his arms willingly, and let his mouth transport her out of this place and the memories and, *worse*, hopeless dreams. Dreams Flora had never acknowledged before.

That evening the event was taking place in London's most exclusive art gallery. It was a huge art auction to raise funds for a collection of different charities. Flora turned to Vito when they were in the vast open space. She wanted to say something to him before he got swallowed up by a steady stream of worshippers.

She caught his hand and he looked down at her. Her face got hot and she momentarily forgot her train of thought. Her blood was still pulsing after what had happened not long ago. When Vito had come into the dressing room after the glam team had left, he'd taken one look at her in the slinky black silk evening gown, and the air had crackled with electricity.

What had happened in the space of the next half-hour had been fast and furious and Flora's nice, neat up-do had sadly come apart and now her hair was wild and untameable and flowing over her shoulders.

She wanted to scowl at him because, while she felt as if what they'd been doing was written in scarlet letters across her forehead, he looked pristine and serene.

He arched a brow. 'What?'

Flora forced herself to focus. He was too distracting. 'I just wanted to say thank you. I got an email from Maria at the women's aid centre earlier and she told me about their new premises thanks to your donation. They will have an acre of land, which will allow kids to bring their pets. You have no idea how much that means…' Flora had to stop, she was feeling emotional.

Vito squeezed her hand. 'After today, I can imagine exactly how special that is.'

Flora looked up at him. She felt as if she were drowning. The connection between them was so tangible, was it really just on her side? Could he not feel it too? Or was she just grasping at straws because underneath the taciturn vengeful billionaire he was actually a person who could be empathetic and that was all?

Before she could wonder too much about it, there was a tap on her back and she turned around to see Carrie Black. Flora was so full of excess emotion and relieved to see a familiar, kind face that she impulsively hugged the other woman. Her husband was greeting Vito. Flora pulled back, mortified. 'I'm sorry, this probably isn't the place for spontaneous bursts of tactility.'

Carrie Black laughed and hooked her arm into Flora's. 'Oh, believe me, I'm just as glad to see you. Let's leave the men to talk while we do some celebrity spotting. I'm sure I saw Harry Styles just now.'

Flora let herself be whisked away by Carrie, relieved to be moving out of Vito's orbit for a little while. She was far too raw after seeing her family home earlier and the explosive lovemaking.

Vito had lost sight of Flora and Carrie a while ago, and he knew his attention should be on Massimo Black, but it wasn't.

Massimo Black said wryly, 'I understand what it's like.'

Vito looked at him. 'What?'

'To be consumed.'

Vito felt exposed. 'By…?'

'A woman. I'd never experienced anything like it until I met Carrie.'

Vito was already shaking his head as if to deny that his relationship with Flora was anything like what this man had with his wife but Black didn't notice and was saying, 'You know, based on your reputation before, I wasn't inclined to invest in your company, but now that we've met and I've seen you with Flora, it's given me a new perspective. To be brutally honest, you can thank her that I'm willing to invest.'

Black held out his hand and Vito realised that this was it. The man was doing a deal, or committing to doing a deal, here and now. Vito took his hand, shook it firmly, feeling a little stunned. 'Thank you, I didn't expect that.'

Black said, 'I don't play games, Vitale. I've no time for it.'

Vito pulled his hand back. His conscience pricked. 'What if…I wasn't with Flora?'

Massimo Black said, 'Then I don't think we'd be having this conversation.'

'So if I wasn't with her, or in a relationship, then you wouldn't want to invest in my company?'

'It might seem old-fashioned but you're a much more solid bet for me if you have cares and responsibilities outside yourself. I don't think you're letting that woman go any time soon, are you?'

Vito thought of letting Flora go, of not having her near him, in his bed, and he felt dizzy. It receded quickly. He just wasn't done with her, that was all. So he could honestly respond by saying, 'No.'

At that moment Carrie appeared by her husband's side and Vito caught an inkling of what Black was saying when husband and wife looked at each other with such intimacy that he felt as if he was intruding.

He cleared his throat. 'Wasn't Flora with you?'

Carrie looked around. 'She was. She just— Ah, there she is.'

Flora approached from behind Vito and he took in her face. There was something about her expression that made him look twice. She was pale. Her smile was forced. He reached for her hand but she was holding her clutch bag. He frowned but had to respond to Massimo Black, who was saying to Vito, 'I'll have my assistant set up a meeting before you leave London?'

Vito smiled. 'Yes, that'd be good.'

Carrie smiled at them both. 'Goodnight, hope to see you again soon.'

The warmth between the women was genuine and Vito had a sense again of how it could be to have someone by his side who could enhance his life in ways he'd never considered before. As Massimo Black had said, if he weren't with Flora, Massimo wouldn't have considered working with him.

And wasn't this what he'd set out to achieve by having her by his side? He'd just never expected that she would be so effective. The other couple had walked away. Vito glanced at Flora and now she looked a little green. He took her arm. 'Are you okay?'

'I have a bit of a headache.'

'Do you want to go?'

She nodded. 'Maybe, if that's okay. You don't have to go. I can get a taxi.'

A sense of disquiet filling Vito now, he said, 'No, it's okay. Massimo Black was the person I wanted to speak to and I have. We can go.'

They walked outside and Vito's driver met them. The journey back to the hotel was in silence. Not like Flora not to be chattering. Vito didn't like it. When they got to the suite, Flora didn't meet his eye. She said, 'I think I'll go to bed in the guest room, so I don't disturb you.'

Vito was pulling off his bow tie. 'Flora, are you sure it's just a headache? Do you need a doctor?'

She shook her head quickly, her hair moving around her shoulders. 'No, it's not that bad, I'll take some painkillers and go to sleep. I'm sure I'll be fine in the morning.'

Vito told himself he was overreacting. He said, 'Okay, goodnight,' and watched Flora slip off her shoes before walking out of the room, Benji trotting loyally at her heels. He felt the urge to trot after her.

He realised that he and the dog weren't all that different. He scowled at the notion and turned away, going to the drinks cabinet to help himself to a shot of whiskey, ruminating on the potential deal with Massimo Black and the fact that having Flora in his life was central to that development.

# CHAPTER ELEVEN

FLORA HATED TELLING white lies. She didn't have a headache. She had heartache, and there was no painkiller for that. She lay in bed for a long time staring up at the ceiling.

She'd overheard the exchange between Massimo Black and Vito, a fluke of hearing her name mentioned and being screened behind a plant. She'd practically heard the cogs turning in Vito's head as he'd all but assured Massimo Black that he was in a committed relationship with Flora.

But then, Flora could hardly blame Vito. At the start of this...unorthodox arrangement, he'd admitted that being seen to be in a relationship would be good for his profile, and also for hers, to restore some of the dignity he'd stripped her of when leaving her standing in that vestibule at the church.

And she knew how important Massimo Black was. If he invested in Vito, it would send him onto another level. The kind of level where his name and business would be immortalised.

Flora wouldn't deny him that. She loved him. She wanted him to succeed. But she also knew that she couldn't continue to harm herself by pretending things hadn't changed, for her. Because she'd fallen for him. She knew Vito wouldn't welcome that, no matter what kind of deal hung in the balance.

Or maybe she was being supremely naive, maybe the ruthlessness she'd seen on that day of the wedding would reappear and he'd have no problem continuing an affair while knowing she was in love with him.

But was she really contemplating telling him? Potentially having him end things, or, worse, being prepared to have him ask her to stay for the sake of his career? Either scenario made her feel nauseous.

Flora couldn't sleep. One thought dominated over everything. It was the more probable likelihood that Vito would end things if he knew how she felt. The thought that tomorrow could be the last day she would see him. Because if she told him, once he knew, that would be it.

Galvanised by a cold dread settling her body, Flora got out of the bed and padded through the suite, lit only by moonlight.

She pushed open Vito's bedroom door. He was sprawled on the bed, bare-chested, sheets tangled around his waist, as if he'd been thrashing in his sleep. Something squeezed in Flora's chest.

She walked over to the bed and, as if he sensed her, Vito's eyes opened. He came up on one arm, hair sexily dishevelled. 'Flora? Is that you?' His voice was husky with sleep. Rough.

She stopped by the edge of the bed. She nodded. 'It's me. My headache is gone.'

*Liar.*

She ignored the voice. She needed Vito, even if it was just one more time.

He put out a hand and she took it, like a drowning woman reaching for help. He pulled her onto the bed and she landed on her back, looking up at him. His gaze roved over her face. She realised he looked pale. He said, 'I was dreaming, that you were gone and I was looking for you and I couldn't find you and—'

Flora put her hand up on his face, his jaw rough with stubble. 'Shh, I'm here. I'm not going anywhere.' As she said that she knew she was putting a nail in her own coffin, because she knew she wasn't going to tell Vito anything for the moment. She was too weak. She wanted him. And she wanted to cling onto this while he wanted her just for a little longer.

Two days later.

Rome glittered under the evening sun, everything bathed in gold. They were in the back of Vito's car being driven to his apartment from the airport. Flora's hand was in Vito's while he took a call on his phone. When he was finished he slid the sleek device into his pocket. He looked at her. 'I'm sorry about that.'

Flora lifted her shoulder in a little shrug. 'Don't be, you're working.' Then she asked, 'The meeting with Massimo Black went well?'

Vito and Black had had a long meeting in London the day before. Vito nodded. He smiled. It made Flora's heart ache—because she was happy for him and she knew she'd never get to see the long-term results of their partnership and friendship.

'We're signing contracts next week. He and Carrie want to take us out to dinner to celebrate. You'll come with me?'

Vito lifted Flora's hand and kissed the inside of her

palm. Her heart rate doubled. Could she hold out for another week? To ensure that Vito's future was secured? When every day she was falling deeper and deeper in love? She forced a smile. 'Of course.'

Vito's gaze narrowed on her. 'Are you sure you're okay? You haven't seemed yourself since the other night.'

Damn him for noticing. Why did he have to demonstrate an ability to read her when her own family, who had taken her in to care for her, had barely noticed her at all? And she was the niece of this man's sworn enemy!

She smiled again, this time not forcing it. 'I'm fine… just a little tired.'

'I don't have any engagements this evening. We could…get a takeout?'

Flora sat up straight. 'I could cook!' Then she remembered that she'd suggested it before and Vito had nixed the idea. She prepared herself to have him scoff at her suggestion.

But he looked at her with an indulgent expression and his mouth quirked. 'That would really make you happy?'

Flora nodded. She'd always loved cooking, ever since one of her uncle's housekeepers had taken her under her wing when she'd been much younger.

Vito arched a brow. 'I'll expect more than pasta arabiata.'

Flora narrowed her eyes on him. For the first time in days she was out of her head and not thinking about the future hurtling towards her. 'Challenge accepted.'

Vito watched Flora from the doorway of the kitchen, a place he didn't frequent all that much. He usually ate out, or had a chef cook. So it was a total novelty to see the woman he was currently sleeping with moving around the space with such dextrous ease.

She was wearing cut-off denim shorts. They must be her own. And a plain white shirt. Her hair was tied up into a messy knot on her head. Bare feet. No make-up. Shirt sleeves rolled up. The buttons on her shirt made his fingers itch to slip them free of their holes, exposing her voluptuous breasts to his hungry gaze.

He diverted his gaze up. She was doing something with rice and breadcrumbs. He asked, 'Where did you learn to cook?'

She glanced at him and back down. 'One of my uncle's housekeepers. A woman called Gianna. She was from Sicily. My uncle used to pay her extra to take care of me if they went away.'

'He didn't even hire a nanny?'

Flora shook her head. Vito felt the all-too-familiar burn of anger towards that man, but then he recalled Flora's hand on his arm in the garden of her old family home, her telling him not to waste his energy. It was slightly unsettling to realise that she seemed to have a way of diluting his anger.

Flora popped a cherry tomato into her mouth. Vito felt envious. Even Benji was lying on the ground just looking up at her.

'You really would be happier here than at a gala function in an evening gown, wouldn't you?'

She looked at him then and a sense of exposure prickled over his skin. She had been off the last few days but here, now, she seemed like herself again. It was mildly disturbing—for a man who had never been around a lover long enough to notice her moods—to realise that he'd become so attuned to Flora.

She looked a little sheepish. 'I used to hate it when my uncle asked me to host parties with him if my aunt was away. I never knew what to do or say. I felt awkward. But going to events with you…dressing up, that was more fun. I didn't feel that awkward.'

Vito shook his head. 'You're not awkward, Flora, far from it.' She wasn't. She was genuine and warm and probably the nicest person Vito had ever met.

She pointed her knife at him and said, 'I hope you're not coming to dinner like that.'

He looked down at the sweatpants he'd put on to work out in the gym. And the faded T-shirt. He looked back up. 'What is the dress code?'

She cocked her head to one side and then said, 'I don't think we need to go full black tie but a suit will suffice. You don't have to wear a tie.'

Vito felt something flip over in his chest. This whole scene…was so seductive. When his parents had died, any such memories of domestic harmony and happiness had died too. He'd clamped down on ever wanting to experience it again. But here, now, he felt a very dangerous sense of…yearning. A sliver of a window was opening up the dark spaces inside him— He shut it down ruthlessly because that way led to loss and pain and grief. He didn't want this. He wasn't in the market for it.

He wondered if he needed to say something to Flora… Was she in danger of forgetting the basis of this relationship?

He opened his mouth but she said, 'Go on, shoo, dinner will be ready in an hour. I don't want to see you until then.'

Vito closed his mouth. Flora wasn't looking at him. She was engrossed in the task. He assured himself he was being ridiculous. Soon enough, she would be getting on with her life, going in a direction that would take her far away from Vito, because he knew their worlds were unlikely to collide again. He waited for a sense of relief that didn't come. Irritation prickled.

Maybe *he* was the one who needed reminding of what this was—a brief mutually beneficial interlude before they both got on with their lives.

Flora adjusted herself in the mirror. She'd showered and left her hair down. Minimal make-up. On a whim she'd picked out a daring bronze silk dress, figure-hugging and with a cut-out over one hip, the ruched silk leaving one shoulder totally bare. It fell to the knee and when Flora put it on she felt sexy and young.

She left her feet bare—what was the point of wearing shoes? But then, she recalled telling Vito he had to wear a suit and at the last moment she paired the dress with gold strappy sandals.

Her heart was skipping beats as she went back to the kitchen to prepare the meal for serving. Ridiculous that this should feel like a date even though they weren't going anywhere. And when Flora knew that even if Vito had lost interest in her, he probably wouldn't admit it until after he'd done the deal with Massimo Black.

But, if how he touched her and looked at her still were any indication, their chemistry was as potent as ever. She couldn't imagine ever wanting a man as much as—

'Well? Will I do?'

Flora looked up from where she was arranging arancini balls onto two plates. Her heart stopped beating. Vito stood in the doorway, practically taking up the entire space. He wore a white shirt and dark trousers that moulded so faithfully to his body that she could practically see his musculature.

His hair was still damp, swept back. Jaw clean-shaven. She caught a whiff of his scent—earth and leather and so sexy that she wanted to close her eyes and navigate her way to him by smell alone.

It was almost as if she'd never seen him before, his impact on her was so acute. Somehow she found her breath and got some oxygen to her brain. 'You'll do.'

He came into the kitchen and that dark gaze swept her up and down. Her skin tingled all over when she saw the appreciative flare in his eyes, turning them molten. *For her.*

He said, 'You look…edible.'

Now her legs wobbled at the thought of him actually— Quickly, before her thoughts could turn into an X-rated movie in her head, she thrust the plates at him. 'Take these through. I'll follow.'

'Yes, ma'am.'

Flora gathered herself and ran some cold water over the hectic pulse at her wrists before joining Vito in the dining room. He saluted her with his glass of white wine. 'To you, Flora. This looks amazing.' He gestured to the table she'd set. She'd picked flowers from the terrace and created a little posy in the centre of the table. She felt embarrassed now for going to such lengths. She blushed. 'It's nothing. Please eat while the arancini is still warm.'

The traditional Sicilian dish of risotto balls mixed with cheese and then covered in breadcrumbs and deep-fried was one of the first things Flora had learned how to cook.

Vito took a bite of one and closed his eyes. He said, 'The best arancini I've ever tasted.'

Flora beamed and blushed even more. 'You're just saying that, but thank you.'

'I'm not. I won't lie and say I have the most sophisticated palate on the planet, but I know good food when I taste it.'

Flora took a bite and when she could speak, she said, 'Your mother wasn't a good cook?'

Vito made a face. 'Not the best, no. And my father had no interest. We lived on a lot of processed food, which I know is sacrilege to most Italians.'

'Sounds like your mother had more interesting things to be doing. Did she work?'

'She did admin for my father a few days a week while I was in school. I think, when they didn't have more children, she resigned herself to her time not being dominated by a larger family, but I knew she was sad.'

'That must have been very tough, because it's only recently that women are opening up more about things like that, and men.'

Vito inclined his head. 'Exactly. Who knows what support she might have received today?'

Flora took a sip of wine. 'You said before that you didn't miss siblings?'

Vito shook his head and sat back, wine-glass stem between his fingers. 'Not really. I can't explain why… I had lots of friends on our street.' He gave a rueful smile.

'I probably liked being the sole focus of their attention, if I'm honest.'

Flora's heart flip-flopped. He constantly surprised her with moments of self-deprecation like this. Originally she'd thought he was a man of her uncle's ilk, ruthless and cold and obsessed with power, but he wasn't like that at all. He'd come by the way of power in his pursuit of revenge, yes, but he was obviously innately talented and intelligent. And, underneath it all, he was kind. He'd taken her in when she was sure he still hadn't trusted her. Maybe he still didn't fully trust her. That sobering thought burst a little of her rose-hued bubble.

She forced a bright smile. 'Ready for the main course?'

Vito nodded. 'That was delicious, thank you.'

Flora cleared the plates and came back moments later with the main, tender fillets of steak with a sauce made from olive oil, lemon, garlic and oregano. Fragrant and tasty. This was accompanied by roasted rosemary baby potatoes and crisp steamed vegetables.

Vito made appreciative sounds as he tasted the steak. He wiped his mouth. 'This is amazing. Did you ever think about being a chef?'

Flora was flattered. She'd only ever cooked for her uncle and aunt and they'd never made a fuss like this. 'I do like cooking, but I don't think I have enough of an interest to pursue it.'

'You still want to do graphic design?'

Flora nodded, swallowing her own mouthful. 'Yes, I was always doodling, even as a child. My mother's father was a pretty well-known artist so it's in the family. The English side, at least.'

'There were no relatives on that side who could have taken you in?' Vito asked.

Flora shook her head, pushing down the old grief and pain. She'd successfully blocked it out for years but it felt so much closer to the surface now, since she'd been with Vito. As if their intimacy was dismantling her defences.

'No, my mother was an only child and her parents died relatively young, too. So my uncle on my father's side was all I had.'

Vito wiped his mouth and said, 'I have something for you.'

Flora was about to ask, *What?* but he was gone, out of the room. He came back a minute later and handed Flora a business card. She read the name of a solicitor she'd never heard of—a specialist in inheritance law. She looked at Vito. 'Should I know this person?'

'You will,' he said enigmatically. 'I've retained him to liaise with you about receiving the inheritance you're due.'

Flora couldn't compute what Vito was saying. She frowned. 'But my inheritance is gone. Spent.'

Vito shook his head. 'I told you that I didn't wipe out your uncle completely. He still has a healthy stash of money. Not enough to start again but enough to live on. I contacted him and threatened him with legal proceedings if he didn't pay you your inheritance plus interest. It's at least—'

When Vito mentioned the amount, in the millions, Flora's head spun. 'I knew it was a lot but I had no idea...' She focused her gaze back on Vito. 'But how...?'

'It'll probably wipe out most of his disposable income, but he knows he can't afford the legal bills, and more importantly he knows that he's in the wrong. He would face the courts for embezzling his own family. The last thing he wants is to face extradition proceedings back to Italy. This solicitor just needs to meet with you to initiate the proceedings that will transfer the funds into your account.'

Flora thought of her uncle and aunt, and her conscience pricked, even now. Vito read her expression and said, 'Flora, I could very easily give you this money, but I know you wouldn't take it. It has to come from your uncle. He owes you this. He should never have taken what your parents left to you—do you think they would want what happened to you?'

Flora recalled that last image of her parents' loving smiles in the car as they'd left her at her friend's house. They'd adored her and she them. Of course they'd want her to be looked after.

The fact that Vito had done this for her… Emotion squeezed her chest and all the way up to her throat, making her eyes sting. No one had ever shown her an ounce of consideration since she was eight years old. Except for this man.

He reached for her hand, visibly concerned. 'I thought this would be a good thing?'

She nodded and tried furiously to blink back the tears and swallow the emotion. 'It is…it is…it's just that no one has ever advocated for me before and I should've been able to do it for myself, but I always felt so guilty when I imagined standing up to my uncle because he took me in—'

Vito reached for her and pulled her out of her chair and

over onto his lap, thighs like steel under her bottom. Her blood heated even in the midst of this emotional storm.

He held her and said, 'That man took you in because he saw an opportunity. He didn't do it out of genuine love or concern. You owe him nothing. He owes *you*.'

Flora said quietly, 'I think when something has been drummed into you from when you're so young…it's hard to let it go.'

'He didn't see you, Flora. He never appreciated who you really were. You deserved so much more, and you have a lot to offer in whatever field you choose to go into.'

Flora looked at Vito, feeling emotional. That was one of the nicest things anyone had ever said to her.

*He saw her.*

The knowledge of that was so seismic and so overwhelming that she had to focus on his physicality to stop her mind from spiralling out of control.

This close she could see the deep fiery gold depths in his eyes. The long lashes. High cheekbones. A fierce swelling of love and emotion swept up inside her. Terrified she might say something before she could stop herself, she pressed her mouth against his, trying to transmit all the emotion she was feeling without revealing herself.

He accepted her kiss and opened to her, letting her explore him as he'd done her a thousand times by now. All at once familiar and wholly new. One of his hands moved to the bare skin of her hip and waist, revealed by the cut-out of the dress. He caressed her there, sending her pulse skyrocketing. Flora welcomed this physical distraction from the emotion. He wouldn't thank her for that. She drew back after a long drugging moment to pull air into her lungs and brain. She looked down. She still felt dangerously emotional and seized on something to defuse it. 'Let's go dancing.'

Vito arched a brow and he moved minutely, leaving her in no doubt about how he was feeling right now.

*Hard.*

'I'd be quite happy to stay in.'

Flora was tempted but she was also afraid she'd reveal herself. She stood up from Vito's lap. She gestured to her dress. 'I think this deserves an outing, don't you?'

Vito scowled. 'I'm not sure if I want anyone else to see you in that dress.'

Excitement sizzled along Flora's veins. She loved his possessiveness. 'I've only ever been clubbing that one night…' She trailed off, remembering what had happened, when Vito had brought her back here and made love to her for the first time. It felt as if years had passed and it felt like yesterday.

Vito stood up and took her hand and said, 'Very well, then, let's go out, but I can't promise that I'll last long.'

Flora thrilled at that. Within minutes they were in the back of Vito's chauffeur-driven car and heading into the city. Flora took in people strolling along pavements, enjoying the balmy evening. Lovers hand in hand. Families with small children, eating gelato.

For the first time in her life, she felt really, truly free. And hopeful for the future, in spite of the inevitable heartbreak she faced. She'd weathered storms before. She would weather this.

*Would you? Really?*

For a second, a sense of utter desolation washed through her at the thought of never seeing Vito again, except in magazines or on TV. The kind of desolation she'd only felt once before, after losing her family.

'What is it? You look like you've seen a ghost. Have you changed your mind?'

Flora shook her head. She needed distraction now more than ever. She looked at Vito. 'I'm fine.' Impulsively she added, 'Thank you.'

'For what?'

'For looking out for my interests when you had no incentive to do so.'

He shook his head. 'I had every incentive, after what I did to you. You deserve it, Flora. You deserve to live the life you inherited.'

'Still… I'm your enemy's blood and you've forgiven me, that's a lot.'

*'I'm your enemy's blood and you've forgiven me…'*

Flora's words resounded in Vito's head as he led her by the hand to a roped-off VIP booth in the nightclub. They'd unsettled him. Made him doubt himself for a moment, and his instincts to trust Flora. Made him wonder if he was being a monumental fool to have believed she was as pure and kind as she seemed.

After all, her social reputation was now restored and she would receive her full inheritance, making her a very wealthy woman in her own right. Would she have achieved this without Vito? Not likely—he was the only one with the ability to turn the screws on her uncle.

Had she orchestrated this whole affair? Vito had to force himself to remember that it was him who had spotted her at that hotel. The hotel owned by him. What were the chances that she would be serving at an event there?

Irritated with himself for allowing seeds of doubt to take root, he ordered a bottle of champagne. He watched Flora looking around, taking in the club and the glamorous clientele. Strobing lights painted everything a rainbow hue of glittering colours. She was smiling, and in this light Vito could almost convince himself there was a satisfaction to it, as if she'd done what she'd set out to do.

He shook his head. Paranoia didn't suit him. It made him feel out of control. He reminded himself that, even if Flora had set out to regain her inheritance through Vito, it was no less than she was due. He wasn't wrong about her cutting ties with her uncle—there had been no contact between them and her uncle's reaction to having to hand over Flora's inheritance had been vitriolic to say the least.

The champagne arrived. Vito handed Flora a glass. She smiled and took a healthy gulp, wrinkling her nose. Then the beat of the music changed and Flora put down the glass and said over the heavy bass, 'Come on, let's dance.'

Vito would have protested that he didn't *dance*, he usually came here to choose a lover and leave. He'd never actually come to a place like this to enjoy the music. But Flora was leading him down onto the dance floor and turning to face him, lifting her arms in the air, swaying to the music. He noticed men around them look at her, and then at him, and then hurriedly away, once they saw his expression. He felt fierce. Possessive. In spite of the doubts he was suddenly entertaining.

He reached for Flora, telling himself that it really didn't matter if she was out to get all she could from this liaison because he would have done exactly the same.

The fact that she might not be all she seemed shouldn't disappoint Vito because he'd stopped believing in myths and fairy tales a long time ago and that hadn't changed.

Flora still felt as if she were floating when they returned to Vito's apartment a couple of hours later. The champagne had gone straight to her head, in spite of the food, and she felt deliciously tipsy. She swayed slightly when she bent down to remove her sandals in the hall and stood up again giggling, one sandal still on. Vito looked at her and then she hiccuped, which made her giggle again. She whispered loudly, even though there was no one to hear them, 'I think I might have had a little too much champagne.'

Vito smiled, but there was something about it that registered with Flora as being *off*, but she was too tipsy to figure out what. She slipped off the other sandal and tossed it aside.

She threw her arms wide and declared, 'Take me to bed and make love to me, Vito.'

He came towards her and said, 'I think we might just get you tucked up for now, hm?'

He swung her up into his arms, and her head swirled for a second. She muttered, 'Spoilsport.' She spied the opening of his shirt and explored underneath with her fingers, caressing his skin.

'Flora…' Vito said warningly.

'Hush,' she said, suddenly feeling quite sober as another type of inebriation took over. Desire. She pulled his shirt aside, undoing a couple of the top buttons to give her access to more skin, and pressed her mouth there, drinking in his scent, tasting his skin with her tongue.

She felt his arms tighten around her. He was walking them into his bedroom now and he placed her down on the bed. Flora looked up at him. He stood for a long moment and said, 'You should sleep.'

But Flora felt no more like sleeping than she did not breathing. He turned and went towards the door. Flora stood from the bed and said, 'Wait, Vito…'

He stopped and turned around. Flora found the catch at the top of her shoulder and undid it, making the top of the dress fall to her waist, baring her breasts. It clung perilously to her hips. She made a minute move and the dress fell all the way off to the floor. 'Oops,' she said.

She could see Vito's body stiffen. Her blood rushed in response. He came back towards her, shedding his jacket as he did. He stood before her, tall and intense. She shivered at the look in his eyes, shivered with anticipation.

'Flora, are you trying to tempt me?' he asked.

'Is it working?'

A muscle in his jaw pulsed. 'Yes, damn you. Are you sure—?'

Flora closed the distance between them and lifted her hands to undo the rest of his shirt buttons. 'Yes, Vito, I'm sure. I'm a little tipsy, that's all. I know what I'm doing and what I want.' She looked up at him as she spread his shirt wide, revealing his chest. 'And what I want is you. *Now.*'

Vito was naked in seconds and tumbling back onto the bed with Flora. She revelled under his delicious weight, his hard planes and surfaces and the very hard evidence of his desire for her. She wrapped a hand around him, widening her legs, inviting him in… The head of his erection touched her sensitive skin, Flora's entire body waited on a bated breath and then Vito huffed a curse. 'You're a witch. I need to get protection.'

Flora hadn't even noticed. She'd wanted Vito that badly. Or had she known on some deep level and been prepared to take the risk? Flora's conscience pricked.

Before she could overthink it, Vito was back and sliding between her legs again, and with one smooth thrust he drove deep into her body, stealing her breath and sanity.

All of the emotions Flora had been feeling earlier and suppressing rose up inside her now. She was too raw to hold them back. As the storm broke over them, too strong to resist, Flora cried out with the pleasure and beauty of it. Her body spasming around Vito's for long seconds, loath to let him go. Legs wrapped around his hips. Arms around his neck. Breasts crushed to his chest.

It hadn't been like that before. She pressed her mouth to his shoulder, tasting the salty tang of his sweat, revelling in it. He went to move, to extricate himself, but Flora said, 'Wait, don't move.'

She had some instinct that she wanted to imprint this memory onto her brain for ever. How it felt to have Vito in her, over her. So entwined that she didn't know where he ended and she began.

And at that moment it bubbled up inside her, the need to tell him, to let him know, and as he said, 'Flora—' she blurted it out.

'I love you.'

# CHAPTER TWELVE

For a long moment there was silence. Then Vito detached himself from Flora's embrace. She winced as sensitive muscles released their grip on his body. He got up from the bed in one fluid athletic movement and went to the bathroom, presumably to deal with the protection.

It gave Flora a second to pull a cover over herself and pray that she hadn't actually uttered those words out loud, that she'd just thought them in her head. But she could already feel the chill in the air, chasing across her skin. Trickling down her spine. There was no hint of inebriation left. She was stone-cold sober.

Vito reappeared, tying a towel around his waist. His face looked blank.

*She'd said the words out loud.*

Flora sat up, holding the sheet to her. 'Vito—' But he held up a hand, stopping her. She closed her mouth.

'What did you just say?'

Flora bit her lip. She could say *nothing* and try to blame it on the sparkling wine and the moment, but everything in her resisted against it. She couldn't hold it in.

'I said I love you.'

He shook his head. 'Why?'

Flora looked at him. 'You want me to tell you why I

love you?' The thought of trying to articulate everything in her head and heart terrified her.

He looked frustrated. He ran a hand through already messed-up hair. 'No, I mean… I don't know. I mean, *how*?'

'I fell in love with you. I didn't plan on it, Vito… I didn't expect it.'

Now he sounded accusing. 'I told you from the start what this was. I never promised anything more than just…this.'

'I know,' Flora said miserably, any faint hope that he might have greeted her declaration differently turning to dust.

'What is this?' he said. 'Are you playing some sort of game? Now you've got your inheritance and you want to see if you can get more? A serious commitment?'

Flora went cold. She felt more exposed than she'd ever felt in her life. And she'd asked for this. She'd revelled in Vito actually *seeing* her, except he hadn't seen her at all. The pain was immense.

She said, 'Can you hand me a robe, please?' She couldn't conduct this conversation naked under a sheet with the touch of Vito's hands still warm on her skin.

He disappeared into the bathroom and returned with a robe, handing it to her. Flora pulled it on while trying not to expose her body. Ha! That horse and the entire herd had bolted a long time ago. She stood up from the bed, tightly belting the robe around her. The fact that Vito's gaze dropped over her body and back up, sending frissons of awareness all over her skin, was like a betrayal now.

She folded her arms over her chest. 'I guess I shouldn't

be surprised that you're still as cynical as you always were. And who's to say that I'll even collect my inheritance? That's tainted money.'

'Flora, that's your money. You can't *not* take it.' And then he muttered, 'You'll probably hand it all over to a charity anyway.'

Flora pounced on that. 'One minute ago you're accusing me of being an opportunist and now you're saying I'll give it away. Which is it, Vito? Who am I really?'

He looked at her. 'That's just it. I don't know.'

Flora looked at him as her insides knotted. She'd believed that he'd seen her. The worst thing was that Vito had an air of defeat about him. Resignation.

*You do know me*, she wanted to shout at him. Grab him by the shoulders and shake him.

But evidently she was the fool here because he was literally telling her that, even now, after all this time spent together, he still didn't trust her.

And could she even blame him? She was a Gavia. And it was always going to come down to this.

Still, she seemed to have some instinct for self-flagellation because she heard herself saying, 'It means nothing to you that I love you?'

His expression had turned to granite. He shook his head. 'I'm sorry.'

Flora needed to escape then, to go somewhere to lick her wounds and take a moment to assess how she could still be breathing. She backed away. 'I should check Benji…we didn't…when we came in. I'll go back to my own room and tomorrow…'

'We can talk in the morning.'

Mere minutes ago, Flora and this man had been so entwined they'd been one person. Now it couldn't be more glaringly obvious that that had been just an illusion.

She turned, and somehow left the bedroom. Like an automaton, she went to check Benji, taking him out to the terrace for a few minutes and then back inside. She carried him to her bedroom and lay down on the bed, with him tucked against her body.

Vito stood for long moments at his window, as the faintest trails of dawn started to light the sky outside. He waited for a sense of relief to start spreading through him—the relief that always came when things ended with a lover. Whether it was after a night, or two nights, or a week. Because a week had always been his limit before. But not with Flora. It had been several weeks. How many? He wasn't even sure. For some reason his brain wouldn't function. It was stuck on a loop like a broken record, a loop of Flora's declaration: *'I love you.'*

She didn't love him. She couldn't.

She'd told him: *'Don't worry, I would have to be the biggest idiot on the planet to trust you with my heart.'*

The fact that he remembered those exact words wasn't something Vito cared to think about now.

The notion that she could have somehow come to trust him enough to give him her heart was unthinkable to Vito. The thought that perhaps she'd seen something in him—something worth loving—made no sense to him. His life had been consumed with revenge and mining his hurt and pain to succeed. He'd lost anything in him worth loving when his parents had died.

But in the first moment of hearing those words, when his body had still been so deeply embedded in hers, he'd not reacted with rejection—he'd felt a blooming sense of warmth, as if he were melting from the inside out.

Her saying she loved him had been a shock, that was all. She'd caught him off guard.

It was as if his brain had just taken a second to catch up, to realise what she'd said. And then he'd felt Flora's legs and arms around him, holding him, and he'd felt two very different impulses vying for supremacy—*Stay, sink deeper, never let her go* and *Go, leave now, run.*

So he'd run. He felt the tension thrumming through his body now. The urge to go. Put distance between them. Put distance between him and those words that even now felt as if they were living breathing things, whispering around him, making him remember what it had been like to bask in the unconditional love of his father and his mother. The feeling of security—that nothing would ever harm them, or their world.

But they had been harmed. And their world had exploded. And everything had been lost. So Vito would never trust that feeling again and he certainly wouldn't succumb to it.

The next morning Flora felt gritty-eyed. She'd showered and changed into her own clothes, faded jeans and a shirt. Hair pulled back into a loose plait to try and tame it.

She felt numb inside. She'd done this. She'd hastened the demise of her and Vito's relationship by revealing her feelings. But maybe it was for the best. She needed to get on with her life. Without Vito.

She went into the kitchen first and attended to Benji, giving him his food. She heard a sound and looked up but, heart thumping, discovered it was just Sofia, who told her that Vito was in the dining room having breakfast.

Then Flora blushed when she remembered the previous evening. 'I'm sorry, I made dinner and left everything—'

The woman smiled and shook her head. 'No problem, it's nice to see the kitchen get some use.' She winked at Flora, who smiled back weakly. The thought of seeing Vito was making her guts churn, but she steeled herself and went into the dining room.

He was taking a sip of coffee and reading something on his tablet. He looked up and Flora instantly felt as wan and tired as he looked fresh and rested. Clearly not remotely heartbroken. But she was determined not to expose herself any more than she already had. Forcing a bright smile, she sat down. 'Good morning.'

'Morning. Coffee?' He held up the pot and Flora held out her cup, hoping her hand would stay steady. It did, as he poured her some of the fragrant drink. Small mercies. She took a fortifying sip.

Sofia came in with fresh fruit and pastries. Flora smiled at her. When she'd left Vito cleared his throat. Flora pretended putting together her granola, fruit and yoghurt was suddenly the most important thing she'd ever done in her life.

'Flora.'

Damn. She looked up. Vito had put down the tablet. He looked…

*Oh, no*, the worst.

She saw pity on his face.

He said, 'Look, last night—'

She put up a hand. 'I don't really want to discuss it.

We said all that was needed. I'll move out today and we can move on.'

'You don't have to move out.'

The thought of living here in some kind of torturous limbo with Vito made Flora shudder. 'I do, but thank you.'

'No, you really don't. I'm going to New York today, within the hour, and then to London. I won't be back for about ten days.'

Flora had just stuffed a mouthful of granola and fruit and yoghurt into her mouth. It might as well have been cardboard for all she tasted of it. She managed to swallow without choking.

Vito said, 'I'm not just going to kick you out. You'll have time to get settled again.'

She knew from past experience not to be too proud. 'Thank you. I'll be sorted by the time you get back.'

'Will you contact the solicitor?'

Flora looked at him, the hurt at what he'd said last night still fresh. 'You mean, instead of trying to lure you into a more serious commitment?'

Vito's face flushed. 'I'm sorry. You didn't deserve that.'

The apology didn't mollify her all that much. 'But you're still not entirely sure, are you?'

'The only person I trust entirely is myself. I'm a loner, Flora. I never claimed to be anything different.'

Even now, Flora's treacherous heart squeezed. This man had so much to give. And maybe he would one day, but not to her.

'You are what you convince yourself you are, Vito. I'm surprised that you would limit yourself like that when you've had no problem breaking any other limits holding you back.'

Flora waited for his response—he was looking at her with such intensity—but then his phone rang and he glanced at the screen. She saw it too—the name *Massimo Black*—and her insides lurched. The dinner date. They were meant to be together.

Vito answered the phone and just said tersely, 'Can I call you back in a few minutes?'

Black must have answered in the affirmative because Vito terminated the call and put his phone back down on the table. Flora blurted out, 'I overheard you.'

Vito frowned at her. 'Overheard what?'

'Your conversation with Black in London. The night of the event in the art gallery. I heard him say to you that if we weren't together he probably wouldn't have agreed to do business with you. And I heard how you…didn't tell him that it was only a temporary affair.'

Vito's face flushed again. 'You think I misled him.'

'Not exactly…after all, we were together. I'm sure you saw no reason to assume we wouldn't still be together until such time as a deal was done. And you never hid that you were intending on using us being seen together as a way to restore your reputation.'

Vito stood up and went to stand at the window with his hands in his pockets. His back to her. She let her eyes rove over his tall powerful form, very aware that this could be the last time. She said, 'I don't think you set out to deceive him, Vito.'

He turned around. 'Still, I didn't make it clear that we weren't in a committed relationship.'

'If you want me to, I'll still come to London with you so he can see us together.'

But Vito shook his head. 'No, I wouldn't ask that of you. If Black won't do business with me for myself then it's better that the partnership ends now. It's not as if we would have been together for much longer, anyway.'

Flora absorbed that little dagger to her heart. Now she knew for sure that this would be the last time she saw Vito. She stood up. 'What I said last night, Vito—'

'You don't have to explain—'

'I know,' Flora said firmly, determined that he wouldn't stop her from saying this. She knew it was just going to add to the hurt, but she needed him to know. 'What I said last night I meant, Vito. I love you. I love the bones of you and the man you are, inside and out. You're a good man. You deserve more than to be a loner and maybe you'll find that some day with someone, because, for what it's worth, I think you'd be an amazing father. I didn't say I love you wanting anything in return. It comes with no conditions or strings. It's just… love.' Flora stopped. She'd already said too much. Vito was staring at her.

There was a long moment of silence and then he said, 'You pay me a huge compliment, Flora. Especially after what I put you through. But I don't…' He shook his head. 'I can't say the same.'

Flora lifted her chin even though she wanted to crumple. 'You don't have to, Vito. You never led me on or promised anything. I just don't want you to think that I said that to extract something from you. I would never do that.'

She bit her lip and then said, 'I believed that you really saw me, in a way that no one has since my family died, but maybe it's good to know that that was just an illusion. Because I know I won't rest until I find someone who can really see me, all of me, and trust who I am. Goodbye, Vito.'

Flora left the room, quickly, before she lost her nerve. She went back to her room and stayed there until she was fairly certain he would have left, and then she emerged to an empty apartment, apart from Sofia and Benji, and set about getting through the rest of that day, and the next, and even though the future stretched out before her like a grey and lacklustre landscape she refused to let it bring her down. She would get through this. She'd been through worse, even if it didn't feel like it right then.

# CHAPTER THIRTEEN

*A week later, London*

'YOU LOOK AS if you're thinking of doing serious harm to someone. Anyone I know?'

Vito looked around at Massimo Black, who was handing him a crystal tumbler holding dark golden liquid. Immediately it made him think of the way Flora's eyes darkened when their bodies joined, glowing dark golden. His fingers tightened on the glass. She'd been haunting him ever since he'd left Rome. Her words reverberating in his head like taunts.

*'I love the bones of you...you'd be an amazing father... I won't rest until I find someone who can really see me... and trust who I am.'*

Vito forced it all out of his mind. He'd been invited here to Black's office in London ahead of their dinner. They hadn't signed anything yet but his conscience rose up like bile in his throat.

He faced the man and said, 'There's something you need to know.'

Black raised a brow. 'Like the fact that you're no longer in a relationship?'

Vito couldn't have been more stunned if the man had

just landed a blow to his gut. He felt winded. 'How do you know?' Had it got to the papers? He hadn't released a statement yet, telling himself he'd wanted to tell Black in person first, but also because another part of him had resisted it.

Black took a sip of his drink. 'Carrie got a phone call from Flora, who wanted to pass on a message to me.'

Black came to stand beside Vito at the window. Vito asked as politely as he could, 'What did she say?'

What he really wanted to ask was, *Was she all right? Where did she say she was?*

He knew she'd left the apartment in Rome because Sofia had told him she'd moved out, with no forwarding address. Was she homeless again? Was she—?

'She said that even though you were no longer in a relationship she hoped it wouldn't affect my judgement of your reputation, and that I'd be a fool to not go into business with you.'

Vito felt a rush of warmth around his chest at the thought of Flora advocating for him.

*'I love the bones of you...'*

He said, more tersely than he'd intended, 'And?'

Black gave him a look. 'I won't lie—if headlines in the paper feature your love affairs over your business affairs, I won't be inclined to continue investment. I favour discretion above all things.'

The bile stayed stuck in Vito's throat. The thought of even looking at another woman or taking another woman to his bed was almost repugnant to him. He muttered, 'I don't think you'll need to worry about that.'

'So why...? If you don't mind me asking.'

Vito chased the bile down his throat with a gulp of

whiskey, and then, knowing he could very well be losing the best prospect of investment he could ever get, he said, 'I do mind you asking, actually.' Because he had no answers any more. He'd been so sure when he'd stood in front of Flora after she'd told him she loved him, but now that certainty was far less…certain.

Black said, 'Fair enough.'

'Do you still want to do business with me?' Vito would prefer to know now.

Black looked at him for a long moment and then said, 'Yes, I do, and this might sound crazy but, even though I only met her a couple of times, I trust Flora's judgement of you as a person. But I won't tolerate bad press going forward, Vitale, understood?'

'Understood,' Vito said, feeling grim, when he should be feeling ecstatic. But all he could think about was the fact that this man, who was little more than a stranger really, trusted Flora more than Vito had.

When Vito returned to the apartment in Rome a couple of days later, he expected that being back in the city would make him feel more settled. After all, he'd just spent time in the two places where he'd so recently had Flora on his arm and in his bed—he'd been bound to miss her presence.

*Her scent, her smile, her infectious enthusiasm, her joy in everything, even the damned dog.*

Vito scowled as he removed his tie and jacket. The apartment felt empty. Like a void. *Lonely.* In all his years since losing his parents he'd never felt lonely. He'd been too preoccupied. *And then obsessed, with Flora.* But now he felt it and it wasn't welcome.

He saw a box on the main table in the reception room and went over. A small black box. And a note. He picked it up.

*Vito, I couldn't seem to take these back. Please accept them now as my thank-you. I hope you find happiness in your life, Flora. And Benji.*

Vito opened the box but he already knew what it was. The cufflinks Flora had tried to gift him in New York. The eagles. Soaring high above it all, with that eagle-eyed vision. And suddenly Vito realised that the landscape below had become very barren and desolate.

*I hope you find happiness...*

It might never have occurred to him that it was a state he wanted to achieve, if he hadn't met Flora. It might never have been something he wanted to aspire to more than professional success. Because it hit him now that, for the last weeks...he'd been happy. For the first time in a long time. Since the tragedy of losing his parents. It had sneaked under his skin and into his head and heart without him even noticing. Teasing him with the possibility that he might have that again, in his life.

It was ironic. The Gavias had got the final word. The final revenge. Because Flora had cursed him, without even knowing it. Because now he knew what he wanted and needed and that the only way he'd ever find it was with her. But she deserved nothing less than his full surrender and the question Vito had to face was this: was he brave enough to admit that, in the end, after all he'd done and achieved, that he was still defeated? Because he hadn't realised until now where true success and fulfilment lay.

* * *

'I love it, Flora, you're a genius.'

'Thanks, Maria, but honestly, I'm not even qualified to be doing this. You should find someone who knows—' Flora stopped mid-sentence because someone had appeared in the doorway of the new offices of the women's aid centre.

*Vito.* Her heart palpitated. She was imagining him. So many times in the last couple of weeks, she'd seen a tall, dark-haired figure only to realise that it was a very poor facsimile of the real man. Maria saw her face and turned around. But Maria knew who he was, of course, because he was funding the charity's new home. Vito was a hero.

Maria went over and Flora could hear the emotion in her voice. 'Signor Vitale, thank you so much. You have no idea how far your money is going to go to help women and children who need a safe place.'

Vito looked at Maria and shook her hand and murmured something Flora couldn't hear. Then he looked at Flora and said, 'It's down to Flora. You can thank her.'

Maria made a half-chuckle. 'No matter what I say or do, she insists on coming here to work for us for free.'

Flora's conscience pricked. Maria didn't know about her inheritance yet and even though Flora had met the solicitor, she'd only taken enough money to find a small place of her own to rent. Maria had offered her board again, but Flora didn't want to take a space that could be given to someone who really needed it. She did have every intention, of course, of donating a significant amount to the aid centre, as soon as she'd got her head around the vast amount of money in her solicitor's bank account with her name on it. 'Don't be silly. It's a pleasure to help. You helped me.'

Maria said, 'What can we do for you, Signor Vitale?'

So far, Flora had somehow avoided making direct eye contact with Vito, but it was as if he was telepathically communicating with her to look at him. She did, and her insides somersaulted. He looked...different. Somehow undone. She only realised then that he was wearing faded jeans and boots. A T-shirt under a light bomber jacket. And that he was holding a motorcycle helmet in one hand. Pink.

He said, 'Flora, can I borrow you for a little while?'

Totally bemused and thrown by the dressed-down Vito and the pink helmet, she said, 'Okay.'

Maria said, 'You've done enough today, go on.'

Flora grabbed her light jacket and pulled it on, following Vito out and down the stairs to the street where a motorcycle was parked, leaning to one side. Some kids were looking at it and scattered. 'Vito...what's going on? Is this yours?' She pointed to the bike.

'Yes, it is, and do you know something? I've never even taken it out for a ride until today. It was a status purchase.'

Flora looked at him. 'But you do know how to ride it?'

'Of course.' He handed her the pink helmet. 'Here, put this on.' Flora took the helmet. Was this really happening? Or was she hallucinating? She put the helmet on her head and Vito—who was now sitting on the bike—said, 'Come here.'

Flora took a step towards him and he fastened the strap under her chin. The feel of his fingers on her skin shot through her like electricity. *Real, not a hallucina-*

*tion.* She put a hand on his and said, 'Vito, what are you doing here?'

He looked at her. 'I just want to talk. Is that okay?'

Flora couldn't speak. She was afraid to ask what about in case it was just to apologise or…ask her if she wanted to prolong the affair even though she was in love with him and he wasn't with her— She shut her whirling thoughts down and took a deep breath and then Vito said, 'Where's Benji?'

Flora found it ridiculously moving that he'd spared a thought for the dog. 'Upstairs in his bed. He had a big walk earlier so he was asleep. Maria will keep an eye on him.'

'Okay, hop on.' Vito held out a hand and Flora put hers into it, letting him help her to swing onto the seat behind him. She couldn't stop herself from falling into the groove of the seat, snug behind Vito. He put on his own helmet and said over his shoulder, 'Put your arms around my waist.'

Flora did so, and found herself slipping even closer to his broad back. The powerful bike throttled to life under them, and then they were off, weaving through the hectic Roman traffic.

It was late afternoon and the city was bathed in golden sunshine. Flora gave up trying to think about what Vito wanted to say or where they were going. She was enjoying the feel of his body against hers and kept her hands tied tight around his torso. She could feel his muscles bunching and relaxing as he drove with sexy confidence.

She realised where they were headed when he started climbing up out of the city onto Janiculum Hill, one of Rome's famous vantage points with amazing views of the city. There was a large car park and a wall where people stood to take pictures or just take in the view.

Feeling very bemused as Vito stopped the bike and got off, Flora let him help her off. She removed the helmet and he took it and put it with his in a carrier at the back.

Flora looked around at the people and the tourist stalls selling hats, water, pictures… ‘Vito…what are we doing here?’

He took her hand and led her over to the wall, a quiet spot. He let her hand go. She looked at him and realised that he seemed nervous. He looked out over the city and said, ‘I used to come here after my folks died, and after everything was gone but the name of the business. We’d even lost our home and were living in a cheap hotel… did I mention that?’

Flora shook her head. But Vito wasn’t looking at her. He said, ‘I know how terrifying it must have been for you to leave my office that day with nothing but the clothes on your back because after my mother died, that’s pretty much all I had too.’

‘Were you homeless?’ Flora’s guts clenched.

‘For a little while, but I learnt to hustle and managed to scrape together enough to get by and find a hostel and then build up from there.’

Flora’s mind boggled at the amount of work he would have had to put in, to start all over again from nothing. Just his name.

He continued, ‘I used to come up here and look out over the city. And I used to imagine your uncle down there somewhere, wining and dining. Living in his palazzo, living off my father’s ruined reputation and business.’

He glanced at Flora. 'Living off your inheritance, although I didn't know that then.'

He looked out at the view again. 'But now, it's someone else who consumes me when I look at this view.'

Flora's heart rate was erratic. 'Who's that?'

He looked at her. '*You*, of course. I'll be wondering where you are, who you're with. Wondering if you're happy. What are you doing? Are you using that money for yourself or giving it all away to the first person who comes along? Because I do know you, Flora, and I do see you. You're pure, and good and true, and kind. In spite of everything that's happened to you.'

Flora shook her head, embarrassed. 'I'm not. You're making me sound like a saint.'

He touched her cheek with a finger, so fleetingly she almost wondered if she'd imagined it. 'You are, compared to me. I let anger and grief dominate my life, crushing all the goodness out of everything. Crushing any hopes and dreams beyond achieving success and revenge.'

Flora couldn't speak. Vito continued, 'But then you came along and showed me how lacking my life really was and how empty my future was. I want a real future, Flora, full of happiness and fulfilment beyond material gains or success.'

Flora felt light-headed. She repeated his words. 'You want a real future.'

'Yes, but it can only exist with one other person. You, Flora. I can't have that future unless you're in it, with me, by my side. I pushed you away because you exposed me for being a coward.'

She shook her head, not sure how she was still standing. 'You're not a coward. You're one of the bravest people I've ever met.'

Vito put a hand on her cheek, stopping her words. 'You're brave, Flora, you're braver than me. When you told me you loved me I pushed you away because I knew that to admit to loving you would mean surrendering everything I've identified with for years—grief, pain, loss, revenge.'

'What are you saying, Vito?'

He smiled but she could see the nerves behind it and the emotion in his eyes. 'I'm saying that I love you, Flora. Adore you. I lasted two miserable weeks before realising there was only one option. To surrender. But it's a happy surrender. I hand myself over to you, body, heart and soul, if you'll still have me?'

Flora looked up at Vito. He was stripped as bare as she'd ever seen him, and she'd never seen him like this. But she was taking too long. Doubt crept into his eyes, his expression started to grow tight. He said, 'You deserve the best, Flora. Maybe you've already realised that and you know that I'm not—'

Before he could self-doubt a second longer, Flora launched herself at him, wrapping her legs around his waist, almost toppling him, but he stayed standing, and wrapped his arms around her. 'Flora?'

'I love you, Vito. No one else would be good enough for me. You're the best. I told you before I love the bones of you and I always will and I want to live my whole life with you.'

She could feel the emotion moving in his chest as he sucked in breaths. 'Thank God. For a moment I thought it might be too late.'

She shook her head and said, 'Never too late.' She bent her head and covered his mouth with hers and a cheer went up from the tourists around them. Flora smiled against Vito's mouth and buried her flaming face in his neck.

Later, in Vito's apartment, after they'd moved Flora's and Benji's belongings back from where she'd been renting near to the new women's aid offices, they lay in bed, bodies cooling in the aftermath of spent passion.

Their fingers were entwined and Flora's leg was draped over Vito's thigh. They were pressed together, and her hair, wild and untamed, flowed over the pillow behind her head. She'd never looked more beautiful and Vito had never felt more content. He'd forgotten what it could feel like. True happiness. It still terrified him slightly but he wouldn't give it up again for the world.

Flora pressed a kiss to his chest and he tipped up her chin with his free hand. He came up on one elbow and looked down at her. She looked at him and smiled. His heart turned over. He said, 'By the way, there was one other thing I wanted to discuss with you.'

She smiled even wider. 'Yes, to whatever it is.'

Vito lay back and smirked. 'That was easy.'

Flora leaned up and hit him playfully. 'What was it?'

Vito grinned. He felt younger. Carefree. He let go of her hand and turned away to the bedside table and took the small black box out of the drawer. He sat up, suddenly nervous again.

Flora sat up too, pulling the sheet up. She looked from Vito to the box and back. 'Vito?'

He opened it and she looked down and he saw how

she paled. She put a hand to her mouth and then looked at him again. 'Are you…is this…?'

He nodded. 'I don't want there to be any doubt… I want to spend the rest of my life with you, Flora. Will you marry me?'

He took the art deco yellow diamond ring out of the box and took her hand. It was trembling. 'Flora?'

She looked at him and tears were brimming in her eyes. She nodded, smiled, and said chokily, 'Yes, Vito… yes, I'll marry you.'

He slid the ring onto her finger and said, 'More tasteful than the first one?'

She half laughed and hiccuped. She threw her arms around his neck and he fell onto his back, happily under her lush body.

'Yes,' she said, 'infinitely.' She kissed him. When she pulled back, Vito tucked some hair behind her ear and said, 'One more thing.'

'Anything.'

'Some day, when you're ready and after you've done your graphic design course—'

'I'm doing a course?'

'Yes, you are.'

She grinned. Vito almost lost his train of thought, especially because a certain part of his anatomy was already coming back to life, but he forced himself to focus.

'You said that you'd like a family…'

Flora went still. 'You said you didn't.'

Vito pushed some of her hair over her shoulder. 'Well, that was before I knew you. I think now that a little girl, with her mother's golden-brown eyes and long wild hair, wouldn't be such a bad thing.'

Vito felt Flora's heart pounding against his chest. She

said, 'Or a little boy with his father's dark hair and dark eyes and his fierce spirit.'

Vito kissed her. 'Or maybe, a little boy with his mother's curly hair and golden eyes and a little girl with her father's dark hair and eyes...'

Flora kissed him and Vito tasted the saltiness of her tears. She drew back. 'Yes, Vito, yes to all of it. I want it all, with you. For ever.'

He flipped them so that he was on top and between Flora's legs. She opened to him and as he joined their bodies he echoed her vow, 'For ever.'

A month later, Rome

Vito stood at the top of the church, waiting. He fiddled nervously with the cufflinks that Flora had given him. The eagles. Flora was late. The crowd were whispering and he knew what they were saying.

*Was she was going to do to him what he did to her?*

The tie around Vito's neck felt tight. He resisted the urge to loosen it. In truth, he'd never felt so exposed, laid bare, as he did in this moment, but he didn't even care. Because all he cared about was that Flora would come to him as promised, even though he deserved every ounce of humiliation she could dish out and more.

*She's not like you...she's a good person.*

He smiled tightly. And then, the crowd hushed and a ripple of expectancy went around the church.

Tension eased inside Vito. She was here. She'd come. She did love him. Music started up. He couldn't help it, he had to turn around. His heart stopped.

Flora stood framed in the doorway, a vision. In a simple white dress, off the shoulder, with little cap sleeves on her upper arms. A structured lace bodice with flowers embroidered into the lace, little pearls in the middle of each flower. It fell in soft tulle folds to the floor. It was simple, whimsical, romantic and very Flora.

Her hair was down, adorned by just a garland of white flowers on the top of her head. The only jewellery she wore, apart from her engagement ring, was the gold necklace Vito had given her. She held a simple posy of white wild flowers in one hand and by the other she held a lead. Benji danced around her feet wearing a white dicky-bow collar.

Vito could see that Flora was nervous, and wanted to scoop her up. She might be nervous, but she was brave. Braver than anyone he knew. And he watched with pride as she moved forward and started walking down the aisle, alone.

When she got halfway, Vito thought, *The hell with this*, and strode forward to meet her. He got to her and couldn't help grinning, his vision blurring a little.

She looked up, grinning too. She said softly, 'Did I have you scared for a second?'

Vito let out a short sharp laugh. He cupped her face in his hands and pressed a kiss to her mouth, ignoring the gasps and fevered whispers and the pointed coughing of the priest. He drew back and said, 'Every day, woman, you terrify me with your goodness and how much I love you.'

She winked at him, but he could see the emotion in her eyes too. She said, 'That's good, because someone has to keep you on your toes.'

Hand in hand, Vito and Flora walked the rest of the way to the altar, with their dog, and committed to a lifetime of love and joy.

* * * * *

*Did you get caught up in the drama of*
"I Do" for Revenge*?*

*Then don't miss these other pulse-racing stories*
*by Abby Green!*

A Ring for the Spaniard's Revenge
His Housekeeper's Twin Baby Confession
Mistaken as His Royal Bride
Claimed by the Crown Prince
Heir for His Empire

*Available now!*